I Married A Reclining Chair... And Other Quirky Tales of Marriage

Lisa M. Fuhs

Genesis Press

Published by
Genesis Press, Inc.
315 Third Avenue North
Columbus, Mississippi 39701

I Married a Reclining Chair...
And Other Quirky Tales of Marriage

ISBN 1-885478-88-7

Printed in the United States of America

FIRST EDITION

Book design by Mary Beth Vickers

Acknowledgements

I would like to thank all of my very patient friends who shared in this book. My best friend, Beth Pfister-Seiglinger, who was kind enough not to throw things at me when asked for the millionth time about sentence structure. My other best friend, Deb Ryan, who sat through many hours of phone calls (and only hung up on me once or twice) while I read and reread (yawn) the chapters to her. Don Thomas, my good friend who donated his cotton ball story, along with a good deal of his pride. My brother-in-law, Dave Gifford. Without his habits this book would have been considerably shorter. And to the many people whose laughter when they read the rough drafts encouraged me to keep writing.

I would also like to thank Gary Frazier of Genesis Press, who took a chance on a brand new author and agreed to publish my book despite the fact that he is, and I quote him, "not the kind of guy" my book is written about. And also Jack Kean, Steve Pieschel, and Mary Beth Vickers for their efforts in getting the book ready for print.

Last, but certainly not least, my husband of ten years, Tim Fuhs. Without him to annoy me, there would have been no book at all.

Acknowledgements

Dedication

Too all of the wives whose husbands fall
under any of the chapters in this book.
This one's for you.

Contents

Introduction

Marriage is not a word. It's a sentence—a life sentence. It is single-handedly the hardest quest you will ever undertake. Root canal? Lead me to the dentist's chair! Major surgery? Piece of cake! Marriage? That's why I wrote this book. There are mornings when I wake up and look at my adoring husband of ten years, who is snoring like the Chicago/Northwestern freight train, drool oozing out the side of his mouth which is gaped open like the Grand Canyon. I roll my eyes and think, *Ugh! What have I done?*

Personal differences (why would I, at five foot two inches, put forty-eight rolls of toilet paper on the top shelf, six inches out of reach, during flu season?), annoying habits (lint ball collections), and disgusting personal conduct (have you ever had to listen to the extremely irritating sound of a man scratching his hairy butt first thing in the morning?) are all part of the compromise (meaning we have no choice but to put up with it) of this blissful (when he's asleep) state known as matrimony.

Men really are from another planet. A planet as yet undiscovered where the high-tech remote control that you would need an instruction manual as thick as a telephone book to operate is always within their grasp. Useless electronic gadgets and toys abound. And farting, burping, and grunting have replaced English as the universal language. By the way, where did all that gas come from? How did he manage to survive all those years we were dating? He must have been in agony! Men have turned passing gas from various body orifices into a refined musical art form.

Male pride is a whole other ball game. Personally, I would rather deal with the gas issue than be on the wrong end of a man whose pride has been wounded. I have spent many a day driving needlessly around, and around and around, while my husband has tried to figure out where he was going, never admitting he was lost. "Put that damn map away! I'm not lost!" he bellows. What the heck is the harm in asking for directions, or simply looking at the map?

Male ego, once it has been wounded, is almost impossible to make amends with. Notice that I have said male ego, not the man himself. As women we rarely remember or deal with the person we actually married, since most of our time is spent dealing with his evil twin known as ego.

The bottom line? Stay away from anything that would hurt the male ego. That limits the topics of conversation to just the weather, but take heart, that won't last long either, since most men will find a way to personalize that too.

There is another part of marriage that women dread the most: cold and flu season. It's the time of year when egos and pride go straight out the window, reducing big, strong men to whining, squalling infants. Automatically a man who can bench press five hundred pounds and run ten miles a day cannot lift the tissue box and is incapable of walking the short distance to the coffee table to get his own remote. Cries of, "I'mmmm siccckkkk," "I'mmmm thirsty," "Where's myyyyy sooouuu-up?" echo pitifully throughout the house whenever the flu rears its ugly head. It's enough to drive a person insane!

I've talked with countless women who all had one story or another to contribute. Some funny and some that defy logic. You might say that this book is our revenge. I made many trips to the rest room while writing this book. Some to avoid wetting my pants and other trips to beat the sink in frustration knowing full well where my fellow trench mates were coming from. I know that anyone who has ever been married or in a long-term relationship with a man will identify with and appreciate these chapters. If nothing more, you will finish this book with a sense of kinship and a feeling that you are not alone.

I have changed names and identifying circumstances. However, due to the predictable similarities between most men and their actions you will probably stop, point excitedly, and scream "Hey! I know that guy! That's my hubby!" All similarities are purely coincidental and indigenous to the male species, which, thankfully, will relieve this author of any and all liability. Enjoy!

Chapter One

Anniversaries, Birthdays and Other Overlooked events

I recently tried to celebrate my ninth wedding anniversary. It started out happily enough, with one dozen beautiful, delicate sweetheart roses, delicious bacon-wrapped filet mignon, and chilled champagne for dinner. All of which was made that much sweeter by the adoring looks I received from the man I married.

I'm not sure when the night began to disintegrate, but I think it started when the grill caught fire while my hubby stood by and watched, saying, "Gee, honey, we have a little fire out here!" Then the roses were squashed in our rush to extinguish the flames, dinner was ruined, and we got into an argument. So much for that milestone in our lives. Instead of nine blissful years of marriage, we should have celebrated nine years without having killed each other. At least this one turned out better than my eighth anniversary, which he didn't remember at all.

Later that night in tears, I picked up the phone and sobbed out my harrowing nightmare of this anniversary to Kate, a good friend of mine in Iowa who then proceeded to top my night by telling me about her first anniversary. She told me that the gift for one's first wedding anniversary is supposed to be paper, and how she had lovingly purchased fifteen shares of Disney stock for her husband, planned an extravagant dinner, donned sexy lingerie, and waited impatiently for him to come home. He came home all right, sweaty and stinky from a hard day at work, forgot that it was their first anniversary, walked right by her on his way to the recliner, and plopped down in the chair, remote in hand, to watch TV. He never even noticed the sexy lingerie! He didn't bring flowers, candy, or a card, and when she told him, sobbing, what the "special" occasion was, and that the gift was supposed to be paper, he marched into the other room, scribbled "I love you" on a sheet of paper, marched back in and tried to give it to poor Kate. She ended up in tears, ordered a pizza, and went to bed, while her insensitive, thoughtless hubby continued to watch television.

Kate and I cried together, and then we got equally hysterical with the giggles, wondering just exactly when our Prince Charmings had turned back into warty old frogs. Why, we asked over and over, can't it just stay the same as it was when we were dating?

Take, for instance, dating versus marriage. Here are some of the metamorphoses that take place:

1. **Selective Memory Syndrome.** When dating, he would have never dared to forget any important thing, including the anniversary of the day we ordered our very first pepperoni pizza. Once we were married, he developed gaps in his memory as big as the Grand Canyon. Now, he is able to memorize the entire Monday Night Football schedule, but forgets more important things, like when we have a play to attend, or the song we danced to on our first date. Once he even forgot that he brought me with him to the hardware store. I had to call a cab to get home. Good grief! Well, it's not quite that bad, but I think you get the idea.

2. **Where Have All The Flowers Gone?** I have been trying to figure this out for nine years. While dating, flowers were customary expressions of his devotion. Now, after nine years of marriage, my husband's flower power has been traded in for a power vacuum, power screwdriver, and all of the other assorted electrical powered items you can use to clean and maintain a household. Gee, honey, thank you! It's just what I've always wanted! NOT!

3. **Wish I May, Wish I Might.** Yeah, right.

You can wish all you want, but it isn't going to change the fact that after marriage he is going to develop the attention span of a five-year-old. You can stand on your head naked while singing the national anthem, and he will just walk by and say, "Hello, Dear! How was your day?" if that. So forget about getting noticed in the new dress, or having him admire your latest haircut. Unless it's a really bad haircut, and then all he will do is make fun of it, so don't expect any words of reassurance. Sexy lingerie, on the other hand, will get his attention, and you won't even have to belt out the national anthem naked while standing on your head. Although that could make your evening quite intriguing.

Birthdays are another sore point. Each year I try not to get my hopes up that he will remember. What is even worse is when he does remember. I cannot believe some of the "gifts" that I have had to endure. Our first year it was a Wham tape. (For those of you who do not remember this mid-eighties group, believe me, you aren't missing much.) The next year it was a pair of purple ear muffs. Another year he overdrew our checking account when he sent me a dozen red roses. The thought was there, sure it was, the thought of winding up in jail for bad checks. One rose would have been plenty. A single red rose, a romantic movie, and dinner out is all I ask. Elaborate gifts are nice, but what I prefer is time. His time.

Does it ring a bell that both Snow White and Cinderella each had a Prince Charming? Now you can stop wondering why both those stories never had sequels. Had they had sequels, we would come to find that Prince Charming is now old, fat, and bald (except for the hair in his ears and nose and on his back), and has never remembered an anniversary.

Chapter Two

Bedroom Boneheads

Romance. Such a beautiful concept, until it gets into the hands of a man. This is one area where men and women have distinctly different ideas. Take for instance my friend Julie, who weighs three hundred pounds. Her husband decided to "surprise" her with an overnight getaway at a pool suite hotel. Julie called me, all excited that the old flame was still burning. Little did she know. After her weekend, she called me in tears. Concerned, I had to pry out of her what had happened. Apparently, when they arrived at the suite, the first thing Julie noticed was that every wall, including the ceiling, was mirrored. It was not her idea of a romantic getaway to see her cellulite dimples from every conceivable angle. Strike one. Upon unpacking, she came out of the bathroom to find a gorgeous box tied with a beautiful satin bow. She opened it and was further mortified when she pulled out a red lace bra and matching pair of panties. Size six, of course. Strike two. Next, her husband whispered seductively that it had always been his fantasy to have sex using the Taiwan basket. Now, for those of you who are naive, like me, this is a basket that hangs from the ceiling of the mirrored bed, and the woman sits in it, and you can use your imagination for the rest. Strike three. Julie finally exploded. I think her tirade went something like this, "*You drag me to a suite of rooms where all I see wherever I look is my big, fat body! Then you have the audacity to buy me lingerie that Twiggy wouldn't fit in! Then you ask me to risk life and limb by hanging from the ceiling over this mirrored waterbed in a basket, while you get your jollies!*" For some reason I suspect that their romantic getaway was anything but.

While I don't weigh three hundred pounds, I am self-conscious of my body, which at thirty-two doesn't look like it did at twenty. Gravity takes over, and all things great and small head south for the winter, and they don't come back. There is nothing worse than being handed a gift box of lingerie by an obviously horny hubby, only to open it and find that you might have fit in it when you were twelve.

Further, while I understand men are more visual creatures, most women do not like to look at their naked bodies, only to be reminded of all of the things that will never be. Get my drift? And as for the Taiwan basket, all I have to say is, "Are you nuts?" With Julie's luck, she probably would have brought the entire mirror down on their heads, or worse yet, gotten stuck in the basket and had to call 911 for an extrication team to free her. There are some places wicker ought not to be.

I have another friend, Patty, who was married to this short, red-haired, overbearing police officer who had a tactless, obnoxious personality and probably a major penis complex to match. She was looking distinctly unhappy one afternoon when we met for coffee. It turned out the reason she was upset was the way Jim was approaching her for sex. With a wry grin, she told me that his way of getting her "in the mood" was to slap her on the bottom and ask, "Hey darlin', you wanna get spanked by Daddy?" In her opinion—and I was quick to agree—this really wasn't very much of a turn-on. We had a good laugh over Jim, and how ridiculous he was behaving, all the while wondering how in the world he could think this was in any way, shape and/or form, sexy.

Better still is my all-time favorite line from my friend in Texas: "Hey Honey! Wanna see my dick?" Gee, if that doesn't get you turned on, I sure don't know what will!

Here's another point to ponder: Why do guys feel this need to name their private parts?

It would seem that they spend enough time thinking about them, they handle them throughout the day in one way or another, they fantasize about using them every chance they get, so it would seem that they don't need to name them. It's like a secret code. My theory is that they name them so that they, and others like them, can talk about their private parts without anyone knowing. My friends and I have had a good laugh over some of the names:

Waldo (As in where is Waldo? As if he'd ever lose track of it.)
Eel (Since it's long and electric.)
UDAMAN (As in "You the man.")
Ernie (My husband's name for his, but when I asked him why, he said he didn't name it. This brought up a whole other dialog in our conversation as to who exactly did.)
Oscar (As in "I wish I had an Oscar Meyer wiener.")
Slappy, Haendel, The Big Bopper (I don't even want to think about why these names were picked.)
Snake (Hopefully it isn't poisonous, unless this might be describing his personality.)
Twelve (Can you tell this guy is lying?)
Woody (Woody Woodpecker, perhaps?)
Andre (As in Andre the Giant.)

I have never laughed so hard in my life as I

did when I had to ask my male friends what they had named their penises. Needless to say, they were more than happy to tell me.

Men are almost as bad at seduction as they are at names. I am allergic to almost every scent known to mankind, and my husband, trying to set a romantic mood one night, lit some candles, played soft music on the stereo, and whispered sweet words of love while giving me an all-over body massage. Then I started to sneeze as I realized through the passion that the air was heavy with the scent of Christmas Bayberry. Sniffling and trying to catch my breath, which he had mistaken for me being turned on, I groped for my asthma inhaler, only to reach over and find that I had my hand wrapped around the actual candle. I finally managed to convey my respiratory distress to my husband, who throughout my ordeal had kept moaning, "Yes, baby, yes!" He was horrified and somewhat disappointed when he realized that my gasps of ecstasy were actually a candle-induced asthma attack. When I asked him why in the heck he had bought a Christmas Bayberry candle in mid-July, he replied that they were half-price at the store. More on his penchant for bargains later.

The great outdoors is not always so great for sex. A friend of mine told me how it had always been her and her husband's fantasy to have sex outside, in the rain, no less. They had been planning it for years. They waited for the perfect rainstorm to frolic amongst nature. The kids were gone and the neighborhood quiet. When they had worn themselves out, they lay breathless, with the raindrops glistening on their hot bodies—and the shiny, three-pointed leaves that surrounded them. The next morning, as she sat hunched over her morning cup of coffee, her husband appeared in the kitchen, member in hand, innocently asking, "Honey, take a look at this." Half-joking she replied, "Please, not before breakfast!" Then she did a double-take as she watched the ugly, red, telltale blisters forming before her eyes. Then she realized that she too felt a certain discomfort. For the record, if you choose to have sex outside, you might want to remember this little jingle, "Leaflets three, let it be!" Since it can be so hard to tell poison ivy from other plants.

Now, this was a difficult subject to write about. After all, we are dealing with the oh-so-fragile male ego, and just exactly where is it the most fragile? You guessed it. The bedroom. My approach had to be balanced just right. After all, us gals do like sex and it wasn't my intention to scare away any guys who might read this. I really don't want to be responsible for rendering anyone impotent. Sexual habits of men and women vary, and so do their ideas of how things should be approached. G-strings do not look sexy on anyone more than one hundred pounds, too small lingerie is not going to rev our engines, but it will leave us wondering why it is revving his. Mirrors in any form are a no-no, and as for poison ivy, I do not need to go any further.

I guess the real message here is that we want to be treated as though he has never made love to us before. We want to be seduced with soft lights, candles (preferably not Christmas bayberry), and romantic music. Scented oils; long, relaxing baths together; and soft words of love, spoken while being held gently in his arms, are the things that turn us on the most.

Chapter Three

Men, Little Boys and Babies

I recently spent an afternoon watching my two nephews, Justin, age ten, and Ben, age eight. What struck me dumb were the obvious similarities between these little boys and most of the grown men that I know. After observing these two kids, I came to the conclusion that men never cease being little boys, or in some cases, babies.

My nephews take great pride and pleasure in trying to outgross each other: "I have bigger boogers!" "No, my boogers are greener and slimier than yours are!" "Are not!" "Are too!" And so on and so forth. They can have contests like this for hours on end, while I look on trying not to get sick. Then the battle over who gets to sit in the front seat of the car starts, and they bicker about this for hours on end, trying hard to compete to see who is faster at making the announcement, "*I get to sit in front this time!*" They also like to throw things at each other. Items like dead bugs, live spiders, something unidentifiable that they found outside. The rule here is the more slimy, smelly, or disagreeable the object, the better they like it as they shriek with glee. Then come the fart and burp wars, followed by hysterical giggling and more toots while they, once again, try to outdo each other. Men tend to behave the same way too.

Case in point: I have a friend whose husband is thirty-four years old and has the worst case of foot odor known to mankind. He knows it, she knows it, and everyone coming into contact with his shoes or socks knows it. One of his favorite activities is to take off his socks and throw them at her, or else he will just hold them under her nose for a minute or two until her eyes glaze over from the rank odor of rotten feet.

Among my preteen nephews, there is also much grumbling about chores, not having anything fun to do, nothing good on television, and by the way, why can't they (stomp, stomp) practice three hundred and sixty degree jumps from a four-foot platform on their skateboards? Call 911 and get the emergency room on standby! While my husband doesn't ride a skateboard, we have made many trips to the emergency room for some incredibly pointless injuries. Twelve stitches to the shin when he fell off the diving board while trying an inward dive that he didn't know how to do, a fractured ankle from running with an untrained dog when he knew that the dog would trip him, five stitches to the skull from popping wheelies on a friend's motorcycle when he had never ridden one before. Which, by the way, was very similar to the injury my nephew suffered at age three, while attempting to pop a wheelie on his big wheel but fell off instead. You get the picture.

Emotionally, I think men stop developing around the age of twelve. That would be right around the time that the hormones kick in, turning them into walking, talking penises, yet leaving enough of the immature little boy in tact so that they can make any future wife climb the walls.

There are even some parts of his psyche that stop developing shortly after birth, namely the parts that take over during injury or sickness. Those of you with kids know the part I am talking about, it's the part of little babies that whines and cries whenever they are ill or injured. Common sense, I am certain, never developed at all in most men. At least you will know you aren't alone in your quest for a grown-up man.

Here are the most common traits shared by men, little boys, and babies:

Babies make a big stink in their diapers. Men

just like to make a big stink.

Babies get upset if they can't find the nipple. Men get upset if they can't get a nipple.

Little boys cover up their mistakes so they don't get in trouble. Men cover up their mistakes so their wives don't find out.

Little boys pout, sulk, and stomp when they don't get their way. Men also pout, sulk, and stomp when they don't get their way.

Little boys shout when they are angry, since they have not yet been taught how to use their indoor voice. Men also shout when they're angry because they have forgotten how to use their indoor voice.

Babies complain loudly when their dinner is late. Men just complain.

Little boys don't like to take a bath. Men simply don't bathe if they can help it.

Little boys like to play with toys. Men still like to play with toys, they just cost more money.

Little boys talk in one-word sentences. Men talk/grunt in one word sentences.

Babies are bald. Men go bald.

Babies are unable to properly dress themselves. Men are unwilling to properly dress themselves.

Babies do not know how to control their bodily noises. Men proudly demonstrate their ability to choose not to control their bodily noises.

Little boys have to be taught to pick up their

toys, and are willing to learn. Men know how to pick up their toys, but are unwilling to do so.

I am reminded of a conversation with my friend Kate. We were watching her sweet three-year-old James, who was plopped down in a sea of bright yellow dandelions, happily picking a bouquet of flowers for his mom. She was melancholy, saying how it was sad that he had to grow up into a thoughtless man like his father. I contradicted her and told her to cheer up. He may grow up physically, but even when he is thirty, he will still remain a little boy at heart. What I didn't bother to tell her was to frame this moment in her mind, since a thirty-year-old toddler really isn't cute anymore.

Chapter Four

Dishwasher Bubbles And Other Not So Helpful Housekeeping Hints By Hubby

This is a subject near and dear to every overworked woman's heart. Housekeeping. Or should I say the lack of shared housekeeping by their spouses. Fortunately, I have never had this problem, since my husband has always shared the housekeeping chores with me—with some really amusing, and not-so-amusing results.

Take for example our honeymoon. In college, and on a limited budget, I splurged and bought a new white t-shirt, white socks, and some slinky white lingerie. Since I was big into pastel colors back then, most of my limited summer wardrobe was pale pink, pastel yellow, white, and peach. In the hustle of trying to get our bags packed and ready to go, my helpful hubby decided to wash *everything* together, including the brand-new, navy blue towels, and my entire wardrobe, along with a good portion of his own clothing. To say we looked like the Smurfs would have been an understatement. Every garment was dyed blue. The photos are hysterical. We are always in blue, except for one or two outfits that didn't make it into the load. Luckily, he did learn from his early mistakes and has since become an expert at getting out spots. He was just a day late and a bottle of Rit color remover short to save our honeymoon.

Now, before I go exalting the skills of my husband the male laundress, I have to bring up one area that needs improvement. He always forgets to take the dryer sheet out of the clothes when they are dry. Now this wouldn't be that bad, except that he once left it in the sleeve of my blouse right before I hurriedly dressed for a business meeting. Sitting with the executives of a large corporation with whom I was negotiating an important contract, I happened to glance down and to my horror discovered the dryer sheet sticking out from the cuff of my sleeve. The others noticed it at the same time, so mortified as I was, I had no choice but to make some crack about how my husband had done the laundry, pull the sheet out, and toss it away. Needless to say, the meeting was pretty much over at that point, since the men at the table were trying unsuccessfully to rearrange their facial expressions into business-meeting serious, but wound up coughing, clearing their throats, and eventually giving in, exploding with laughter. Thanks again, Tim.

Other areas took more work. For instance, just the other day, I woke up to the sound of the dishwasher being loaded, so I cuddled up to my pillow and went back to sleep, happy in the knowledge that I wouldn't have to face a mountain of dirty dishes when I woke up. I was awakened a few minutes later by the sound of Tim (I won't repeat what he said, as it isn't fit for print) yelling at the dishwasher. Panicking, I jumped up and raced into the kitchen, only to step ankle-deep in soap bubbles. Somehow, he had inadvertently used the dish *washing* soap, instead of the *dishwasher* detergent. I laughed until I screamed, and he had a long morning muttering, swearing, and scooping up the bubbles from the floor and out of the dishwasher. Mean-spirited person that I am, I relaxed with a good book.

I hear the same complaints from wives over and over: He won't do the dishes, he leaves his smelly socks lying all over the house, he won't help with the laundry, he won't vacuum or mop the floor, and the list goes on. I have suggested to several friends that they need to stop picking up after their man. After all, just how long can you wear the same pair of underwear, until either you or the other people forced to be around him are gagging? I figure that when the undies get up and beg to be washed, he might get the hint. Otherwise, this type of cure for housework phobias may also work twofold: If he *is* trying for a world record on how long one can wear the same pair of briefs before they have to be surgically removed, then you probably won't want to cuddle up for a little one-on-one with him. So you see, even if he is relentless in his pursuit of looking like Pig Pen from the Peanuts cartoon, he will cave when sexually deprived for a couple of weeks. Trust me. Try it. You may be surprised at how well this works.

Speaking of laundry, Bob (yep, the Romeo who gave poor Kate the piece of paper with "I Love You" written on it for their first anniversary), was in charge of the entire household when Kate had major back surgery. In her absence, he thoughtfully piled all of the laundry on her side of the bed, and slept on the other. When she came home, her side was piled sky-high with clean laundry, unfolded of course. He ended up with this little, tiny space to sleep in. Bob also has the annoying habit of making only his side of the bed. He flatly refuses to make Kate's side. I am still trying to figure out the logic behind that one.

I asked several friends to complete this sentence with regard to their hubby's housekeeping habits: My husband...

Uses a dish, and then doesn't wash it, just rinses it off to use again.
Won't put clothes in a hamper, but he will put it over the top of the hamper in case he needs something.
Won't flush the toilet at night.
Won't throw anything out, he just saves it in one big pile for everyone to trip over.
Has the battle royal with me over running the vacuum cleaner. He will deliberately do the vacuuming half-assed just so I end up doing it myself. Then he gets mad at me and goes to sulk, so that he can play the victim, and avoid having to vacuum.
Sits naked on my favorite chair and then farts, so I am always disinfecting it.
Puts things where I would never guess to look for them.
Leaves his whisker clippings in the sink after he shaves. (Ick.)
Never wipes the toothpaste out of the sink after brushing his teeth.
Has forgotten where the garbage is, preferring instead to stack milk cartons, cheese wrappers, and other kitchen trash on the counter for me to throw away.

Why do men have to behave this way with regard to housework? Long past are the days when a woman's work is in the home. While a woman's work is never done, a man just never does any housework. I vote to strike. Let him eat off of moldy dishes, wade knee-deep in the dirt and lint on the carpet, and live with overflowing trash. I for one do not want to be married to a thirty-five-year-old child. Even a four-year-old can sort socks and perform simple tasks. He is as capable as I am of doing chores. He won't keel over from sweeping. Dusting won't bother his allergies any more than it bothers mine, and as for dishpan hands, trust me, he will recover. So pass along the broom, dustpan, and mop to your headstrong hubby, relax in a hot bubble bath, but don't forget the earplugs so you don't have to listen as he loudly voices his displeasure. If that doesn't work, consider divorce, but make a pact to yourself that you will include a "chores clause" in the prenuptial for your next marriage.

Chapter Five

He Hid The Toilet Paper! Among Other Really Annoying Personal Habits

Scratching, leaving the seat up, admiring what came out of his nose, and keeping a lint-ball collection. These are some of the more tame habits I endure. There are as many annoying habits as there are men to invent them, and just when I thought I'd heard them all, along comes one that defies logic. Among the really annoying personal habits I have had the misfortune to personally experience: slimy, soapy hair balls stuck to the side of the shower; picking his pimples and showing it to me (or worse yet, asking me to pick his pimples); cleaning his four false teeth at the dinner table, or showing his four false teeth to children; the always popular leaving the toilet seat up (I've had my butt dunked in an ice-cold bowl more than once in the middle of the night); not replacing the roll of toilet paper and invariably leaving me trapped on the toilet; and scraping the prongs of his fork on the dinner plate. (This makes my teeth hurt and my hair stand on end.) The endless list of irritating habits goes on and on and on and on. Sound familiar?

I have dedicated this chapter specifically to any woman who has ever had the dubious pleasure of marrying a man who loves to hide things. Here is an important point I would like to bring to your attention: Men, as a rule, are tall, women are short. So *why* do they always have to put important items on the far reaches of the top shelf? Now, who in their *right* mind would store forty-eight rolls of toilet paper on the top shelf, just out of reach, during flu season? Especially since we never, ever use that shelf. (I'll elaborate on this story in a minute.) It's exasperating. If you noticed, I am stressing the "right mind" part. Why do we put up with this? I'm not even going to try and touch that one.

The following stories are true. Unbelievable at times, but entirely true. Names have been changed to protect the not-so-innocent. If you were one of the unfortunates who contributed a story, you have my sympathies. If not, you might want to consider yourself lucky. If you have something worse to tell, I'd love to hear from you. So get out your stress balls, punching bags, dartboards with his picture in the bull's-eye, shots of tequila, or anything else that will help get you through this chapter. Grit your teeth, and proceed with caution. You have been warned that it won't be pleasant.

Now, most of us are familiar with the side effects of the stomach flu, but as bad as the flu is, one of the worst things that can happen to you is to be caught, literally, with your pants down, without a single square of toilet paper. What makes this even worse is that the man who vowed to take care of you in sickness and in health was the person responsible for your oh-so-unpleasant plight. If this sounds really, really familiar, you are not alone. This is what my husband did, bless his six-foot-tall heart, right in the middle of cold and flu season.

I was in the middle of a serious bout with the flu, and had it coming out both ends. I was going through toilet paper like crazy, and was so sore from the diarrhea that I could hardly walk without tears. Right after one extremely wrenching bout of the squirts, after the cramps had subsided, and I had caught my breath, I glanced over and saw that (*aaaccckkkk!!!*) I had completely run out of toilet paper. Not a single, solitary square left. I knew we had about forty-eight rolls since I had stocked up only a few days before, but try as I might, I couldn't find them.

Waddling around, with my pants bunched around my ankles, I finally looked up and, with a growing fury, saw that they were all neatly stacked on the top shelf of our hall closet. You all know that shelf, the one he loves, but you cannot easily reach, even with a fire department cherry picker.

Here I am, with major stomach cramps, hopping up and down with my pants around my ankles, trying desperately to reach just one stupid roll of toilet paper, which seemed to be mocking me, just about six inches out of the reach of my grasping hand.

Luckily for me, but not so lucky for him, my husband walked in at that very moment. In tears, and incoherently babbling, I pointed to my southbound pants, then gestured to the just-out-of-reach toilet paper. Trying to hide a ball of laughter, my husband easily reached up, grabbed a single roll, and very generously offered it to me. Oh, gee, thank you!

After I had sufficiently recovered, I threatened him with life and limb if he ever pulled that kind of a stunt again. I also decided that when I built my new house, I wouldn't have any cabinets made higher than I could reach. I also thought about hiding the Charmin on him the next time he got the flu, just so he could see how very funny it really was.

Now, today that story is kind of funny, as long as the toilet paper stays within my reach. There really aren't many things more aggravating than being stranded on the john.

My husband also has some other strange and unusual habits that drive me right up the wall. For instance, he saves lint balls. No, it's not a misprint, he actually *saves* the lint from the dryer. No, he hasn't given me any explanation, at least not any *reasonable* explanation. He simply loves to do the laundry, for which I am eternally grateful, but one day I discovered that he had been saving lint balls. Not just one or two, but a whole huge bag of lint balls. Thinking that he would have some noble explanation, such as keeping them so that the birds could build softer nests, I decided to ask him. He had no explanation for doing this, he simply started saving them. For no good reason. Now I am starting to wonder just how strange he really is, and if there are any other weird, hidden quirks I don't know about. Oh well, if keeping a lint-ball collection is the worst thing he does, I guess I can consider myself lucky.

The consensus among my married friends is that butt scratching is the most maddening habit of all, sound-wise that is. Bodily functions do not count here, as they are in a class, and a chapter, all by themselves. Most men have this uncontrollable urge to stand at the foot of the bed and scratch. It's a sensation comparable to the raw nerves one feels when forced to listen to nails being raked across a chalkboard.

My husband was blessed with more than his fair share of excess body hair. Blessed, that is, because he can now be ten times more infuriating with the sound he makes when he scratches. It is ten times louder than the sound an average-haired man can make. He has this really exasperating habit of getting up first thing in the morning and standing by the edge of the bed, scratching his hairy butt for what seems like an eternity. *Agggghhhhh!* It is the most obnoxious sound I have ever heard! I have tried everything, including putting a pillow over my head and plugging my ears, but it is the type of sound that just grates and echoes in your head all day long. It has gotten so bad that I really have to work to bite my tongue, just to keep from hollering at him out of frustration. Some days I beg him to please go into the bathroom if he insists on all of that scratching. Most of the time he just ignores me, grins this evil little grin, and keeps right on going.

Speaking of irritating sounds, my husband also loves to rake his fork over the plate while eating. I have very sensitive ears and this just makes my teeth hurt! I have pleaded with him not to do this, but he just won't stop. It had gotten so bad that I finally switched to paper plates just so I could get through a meal.

What is it with infuriating their wives? Some days I swear I married a ten-year-old, not the thirty-four-year-old man I know he can be if he tries really hard.

I guess I am lucky to just have a scratching

problem to cope with. My good friend in Wisconsin has a problem with her hubby sneezing, and soaking everything in his path. He has no self-control and has been known to drench the dashboard of the car, her, or any other unfortunate person or inanimate object in the path of his proboscis. *Ick.*

Another good friend, married six years, has been bordering on the edge of insanity, thanks to Disney. Since the release of the movie *George of the Jungle* her hubby has been going around singing the theme song over and over. She's ready to kill him, or barring physical violence, a divorce would be nice. It wouldn't be so bad, but last week she told me that he's now also belching it out, and pounding his chest to get the rest of the burps to come up. I think I'm gonna be sick. Don't our guys ever grow up?

Another nemesis is Jim Carrey. Just ask any woman who spent several months trying to break her husband of talking through his butt hole. Remember the first *Ace Ventura* movie? My husband loves Jim Carrey movies. He could watch them for days on end. Should I be concerned, at this point, about his mental status? Anyhow, right after watching *Ace Ventura, Pet Detective*, he developed this seriously irritating habit of saying "Allll righty then!" to everyone. Store clerks, employees, me...you name it. It's just so embarrassing, since most people look at him like he's lost his mind. At least I can be grateful that he doesn't bend over and respond by talking through his butt in public anymore. No, he saves this one for me, when we are in private. I've tried to tell him that he's acting like an idiot, but he thinks he's being *soooo* funny. I've reached the point where I'll just excuse myself when I see one coming and walk away. Short of taking away the Jim Carrey movies, I really don't know what else I can do. I thought it was just a phase, but it's gone on for several years now.

Telephone etiquette is another area that needs some work. I have several friends whose hubbies are decidedly annoying when they try to talk on the phone. One of them will get on the phone and her hubby thinks it's a great time to mix a drink in the blender. One guy always puts his two cents worth into the conversation. This can alternately be annoying and funny, since he insists on ad-libbing on the only side that he can hear. Another friend puts up with her husband's loud radio, which seems to get louder as her conversation progresses. After a while, in exasperation, she will yell, "Mark! If you have to listen to that while I'm on the phone, put your headphones on!" Hmmm...this sounds very similar to what little kids do when their moms try to talk on the phone. It must be our husbands' need for our constant attention that causes this type of behavior.

We can all agree that hidden in every man is a child who delights in being as annoying as he can. The most we can hope for is that someday even our boys will grow to become men. More specifically, men who will never irritate their wives, never watch a Jim Carrey movie for the express purpose of imitating him, and never, ever scratch their asses. Hey, leave me alone, I'm enjoying my fantasy.

Chapter Six

NOSE HAIR, BACK HAIR, EAR HAIR

It's a known fact that nearly all men, as they age, lose most of the hair on the top of their heads when it migrates to various places, such as the tips of their ears, their noses, and their backs. Male-pattern baldness and excessive body hair have been the topic of hysterical laughter, and the butt of many jokes among women, probably because men have set such a double standard for us. Take for example a middle aged man who has these really disgusting tufts of hair protruding from the tips of his ears and his nostrils. Why are we expected to live with, and yes, *kiss* a man who has two inches of nasal hair sprouting from his nose, and who looks as though he forgot to take off last winter's ear muffs? Talk about grossing someone out! Do you really think he would be seen in public with you if you had an unsightly tuft of hair sticking up from the tip of your ear? I think not. Or if you had two inches of nasal hair sprouting from both nostrils? Oooooh baby! Pucker up! Last, how about if you had enough hair to weave a blanket, growing all over your shoulder blades? To suggest simple, painless remedies like hair removal creams or waxing would result in divorce. Most men won't touch them with a ten foot pole, preferring to gag everyone within visual range by their excessive, unruly, and strangely placed body hair. Yet all I have to do is stop shaving for a couple of days and then watch chuckling as he recoils in horror, staring at the quarter inch of stubble on my legs, refusing to be seen with me at the beach until I shave it off. Double standard? You got that right, sister!

One year, completely repulsed by his nasal hair, I did break down and buy my husband a nose-hair remover. It's kind of like a little weed whip for your nostrils. It was well received, having been an electronic gadget, of course. Might I suggest that some brilliant, creative individual invent an electronic gadget that would dispense the hair-removal cream for his back? Marketed just for men, with lots of pointless buttons and dials, it would be an instant success.

Oh, and God forbid that you should insult anything about his appearance: "Sorry dear, but I just wanted to tell you that your eyebrows look like Albert Einstein's because you haven't trimmed them since New Year's Day—three years ago!" My husband really does have eyebrows that Albert Einstein would have been proud of. When trimmed, his uni-brow resembles a caterpillar. When allowed to grow out of control, which is most of the time, it can reach lengths of up to two inches long. *Eeeeeewwwwwww!* It has gotten so bad that the beautician who cuts his hair has started offering to mow his eyebrows.

"Wrap heads" are a whole other story. These are men who have lost the hair on the top of their heads, and instead of admitting it, they try to cover it up, only to succeed in looking all the more phony and ridiculous. Guys, if it ain't there, it ain't there. Here's the scenario: The guy grows the sides of his hair long, so that he can wrap it turban-like over the top of his head, spray it into place with an entire can of industrial strength hair spray, and look (so he thinks!) like he isn't bald. Well, I've got news for ya mister, you ain't foolin' nobody!

While wrap heads are bad enough, toupees are worse. Even the expensive wigs—oops, excuse me, toupees, hairpieces, etc.—look awful. Men who wear toupees might as well go out and find a roadkill to glue on top of their heads. I just roar with laughter over those commercials where the man and woman are on a date for the first time, and she runs her fingers through his hair, only to have the toupee fall off into his soup. I have this uncontrollable urge to pull off every toupee that I see.

I also have a big problem with men dying their hair. Now, I know this will cause some controversy over double standards—but hey, if the guys can have a double standard, so can we. The problem isn't that I am against men trying to cover up their gray, I think that's a great idea. Nor am I actually against men trying to look more youthful. The real problem, as I see it, is that men do such an appalling job of coloring their hair that, in most cases, dark-haired men end up looking like an embalmed version of Charlie Chaplin, with their twelve hairs dyed jet black, while blond men wind up looking like an over-aged Beach Boy. With any dye job, less is more. If only men would realize just how dignified salt and pepper hair is! My former boss would take his bottle of hair dye and comb it through his hair, *at his desk*, during lunch. Everyone would double over when he walked by because he would have hair dye staining his ears, and the color did not match the rest of his hair. I am not kidding. He would have jet black sideburns and brownish-black-gray hair everywhere else.

While many men think they look sexy and youthful, many women think they look just plain silly. Personally, I would prefer to see the gray hair or a bald spot, rather than run my hand through an entire bottle of hair spray, or having a toupee fall off in my soup. Here's another news flash: A lot of women think gray and bald are sexy. So men, toss out those toupees, cut that long hair on the side of your head, and be proud of your bald spots! If every hair-challenged man would do that, then I guess we would have to find something else about the male gender to point and laugh at.

Chapter Seven

Pull My Finger!
What *IS* Their Obsession With Farts?

My very first introduction to the old "Pull My Finger" trick was given to me by Dave, my sister's future fiancée. I was eleven years old, and can still remember how mortified I was when I enthusiastically gave that finger a tug, causing this loud, earthshaking fart—or so I believed at the time. For a while, I thought it was hysterically funny. Now, all grown up, I realize why my sister had this pained look on her face.

Men never grow out of their childhood obsession with flatulence. My sister and I laughed until we were doubled over, with tears squirting out of our eyes and running down our faces, over the title of this chapter, since "Quick! Pull my finger!" has been a catchphrase throughout her entire marriage. I felt that it wasn't fair to do this book without giving my brother-in-law Dave at least an honorable mention in the fart department.

When my sister informed him of the title of this chapter, he stopped what he was doing, stared thoughtfully off into space for a moment, and said, completely bewildered, "Why would she name a chapter after Justin?" Justin is his son, my sweet, adorable, as yet unmarred by annoying male habits, ten-year-old nephew. Gee Dave, I wonder who passed along the old pull-my-finger tradition to him, huh?

In addition to the old pull-my-finger trick, there is the "Let's hold her head under the covers after I fart" trick. Oh yeah! That's a laugh and a half! Being restrained, unable to take a breath, under a stuffy blanket, all while trying not to pass out from the noxious fumes. Sounds like my kind of fun. NOT!

There must be a secret class taught in elementary school just for little boys on the art of passing gas. It has to be some type of art form to them, as they can discuss technique and style for hours on end, even going to great lengths to demonstrate for each other just how much squeeze is needed in order to develop a particular sound effect. Oh, and let's not forget those not-so-scientific discussions about just the right combinations of foods to produce a certain stench. How about just the right blend to produce those farts that light up the best? We can't forget that one now, can we?

I had a friend in high school who bent over

and tried to ignite his farts in the locker room with a cigarette lighter. He wound up in the emergency room with all of the hair burned off of his backside, and second degree burns to his bottom. Will they never learn???

Actually, most women would like to forget this entire subject, but the little boys we married just won't let us, no matter how hard we try. This seemed to be the one chapter that women had the most opinions about. It struck a nerve somewhere in the olfactory glands, and they just needed to air their grievances. Horror stories, near death from suffocation experiences, and humiliations were plentiful when discussing the subject of their gaseous guys.

A poll of wives resulted in the following as the top ten types of farts:

1. **The Silent & Deadly Fart.** This creeps up on its unsuspecting victims. Guaranteed to clear a room with a single whiff, silencers are usually deadly in potency. You can always figure out who did it by looking closely at all the males in the room to see which one isn't gagging, and by the way he is trying to conceal a ball of laughter. If he ain't a gaggin', he did it!

2. **The Pork & Beans Fart.** This one usually occurs after a picnic or other occasion where this revolting dish is served. I have nothing against pork & beans, mind you. It's the after effects I dread. The odor is intolerable, kind of like a freshly squashed, fermented bean

being shoved under your nose, and the repercussions almost always last an entire evening—an evening that he spends alone! My only recommendation for this type of fart is to buy him some Beano, and/or forbid him to eat pork & beans.

3. **The Fart & Giggle.** This is when he lets out an especially noisy fart and then giggles like a ten-year-old about it. Hehehehehe! At these moments, as you roll your eyes, you are reminded just how immature your beloved is.

4. **The "I Crapped My Pants" Fart.** This means payback time for us wives. It is truly funny when he farts just a little too hard and then gets a panicked look on his face and makes a beeline for the bathroom. This is one we can just sit back and enjoy!

5. **The Colossal Colon Blow Fart.** The granddaddy of all farts. This type of fart can literally be heard for blocks. Shaking the ground and rattling the windows, it's the fart that contest winners are made of. Potency is irrelevant, as sound is its trademark.

6. **The Fart & Run.** These cause us wives considerable embarrassment. Picture the scenario: generally taking place in a grocery store or other fine department store (if you can get him into one), bored hubbies will let one rip, and giggling, run away, leaving you standing there all alone, looking as if you did it. He will slink back a few minutes later, after the smell

has dissipated, looking very satisfied with himself. The only redeeming part about this type of farts is that most women are on to this trick and, while some shoppers will shake their heads, point at you, and hold their noses, other wives will take one look at the back end of your hubby beating a quick retreat, and they will know exactly what happened to you. If you look closely, the next time you're in the store, you will probably be able to spot a fart & run right away. Just look for a snickering man walking as fast as he can away from a red-faced wife. One note of caution: If you do spot one of these in progress, don't go into the area he just vacated for a couple of minutes.

7. The "I Gotta Go! Right Now!" Fart. If your man yells this while holding his butt, get out of the way fast! Usually coming in clusters, these farts smell just like a port-a-potty on a ninety degree day. Men, when it comes to holding it, have no self-control. If ignored, this fart could quickly lead to an "I Crapped My Pants Fart". Live and learn I guess.

8. The Supersonic Butt-Blaster Fart. Sharp in sound and velocity, this fart is enough to lift your man off the couch, blow holes in walls, or if you have the misfortune of standing behind him, knock you into tomorrow. It's the fart hemorrhoids are made of. Painful when expelled, they are not pleasant for either party.

9. The "I Can Tell By The Smell" Fart.

You've heard the old saying, "I can tell by the smell, he ain't feeling well"? That's what these farts are all about. Indescribably offensive in pungency, they are a signal that you are about to exchange your hubby for a whining, squalling infant. Yes ladies, the flu is about to begin!

10. The Juicy Fart. This is almost always mistaken for an "I Crapped My Pants" fart, but is harmless. It just sounds awful. Squishy, hot and wet sounding when he lets one rip, it is usually accompanied by a repulsive stink, and an exclamation of "Ouch!" from your hubby. I am nauseous just writing about it.

Those, my friends, are the top ten farts. Farts, like annoying habits, are as varied and plentiful as there are men to invent them. All we can do is hold our noses, and hope we don't pass out before we are clear of the damage path. Why men think breaking wind is funny I will never know. Why men think farting for the express purpose of embarrassing or suffocating their mates is even funnier, I will never fully understand, nor do I ever desire to.

One last note. If you can't beat 'em, eat a can of beans and join in! Possibly a whiff of their own medicine will solve the problem.

Chapter Eight

I Don't Need A Map! I'm Not Lost!: Highway Horror Stories

If it has tires or testicles, it's bound to be trouble. For all of you who have had the pleasure of being stuck in a car with an arrogant macho man who is quite obviously lost, or have had to encounter a male driver at his dubious best, you'll know what I am talking about. For example: You know he's lost, he knows he's lost, and the gas station attendant that he has passed for the twentieth time in the past two hours knows he's lost. He's not fooling anybody but himself. To suggest a map results in outrage and indignation by your obstinate hubby. So you drive, and drive, and drive, and drive, until one of two things occurs: He wises up and finds his way, or he runs out of gas. The most obvious solution would be (God forbid) to stop and ask for directions. Even more exasperating is that all he has to say for himself as you drive for hours on end searching for the elusive destination is "We're not lost honey! We just haven't found what we're looking for yet!" Yep. He's a barrel of laughs all right.

Male driving habits are a huge sore point among women. It seems as though most men take great pleasure in one-upmanship, especially when it comes to female drivers. It is particularly frustrating to be sitting at a stop sign, when it's as plain as day that it's your turn to go, and have some presumptuous man, who is in love with himself and his car, cut you off cold. If you dare even look his way you get the finger. This happens all the time. It's as if they are saying, "No way am I going to let some bitch go first! Arrr! Arrr! Arrr!" Why do they have to behave like this? They just end up looking like the nitwits that they really are.

In their defense, I will say that once in a blue moon I will run into a very polite fellow who will graciously wave me on, allowing me to go ahead of him. Miracles do happen. But if your hubby is one of these obnoxious drivers, I would recommend trying to make some type of apologetic gesture to the gal he has just cut off, something to the effect of, "I am sorry that he is such a jerk, and that I am actually being seen in the same car with him!" This way you are not apologizing for him, but for having allowed yourself to be seen in the company of such a discourteous, self-centered ignoramus.

Being a relatively good-looking person, I have also experienced young and old male drivers who rev up their engines, weave in and out of traffic, and squeal their tires, all in the spirit of trying to impress me. Sometimes I have to restrain myself from openly pointing and laughing at them, but I have found a sure-fire deterrent: I pick my nose. This is guaranteed to stop such behavior right in its tire tracks, so to speak. So the next time you'd like to get rid of a man who is acting like a sixteen-year-old cruising for chicks on Saturday night, try picking your nose, it works wonders.

Men think they know everything about driving a car. Ha! That's a laugh and a half! Statistics show that hotheaded or drunk *men* cause the majority of car accidents. Personally, I have been in seven accidents in my lifetime, none of which were my fault, and six of which were caused by men. I was rear-ended by an impatient *man*; broad-sided by a *man* who ran a red light because he didn't have any brakes on his '59 Chevy Bel Air; hit head on, at low speed, by a *man* who crossed the centerline; it was a *man* who backed into my newly repaired (from my husband putting us in a ditch during an ice storm) truck, and bashed in the front end. Last but not least, it was a *man* whose manure spreader bounced out of his truck and hit my car door, rendering it useless until it could be repaired. After this accident, the man threatened to physically hit me, and ignored my request not to move his truck until the police could get there. When the police finally did arrive, he pointed to the manure spreader, now all crushed and covered with the white paint from my car and sitting innocently in his truck, and tried to tell the officer that the damage to my car had been there all along. Luckily, there were two witnesses who stopped. So I could prove that this man really was lying. It also helped that the officer was a woman who, contrary to popular belief, did have enough brains to figure out where the fresh damage came from. Doesn't that sound just like a man? The latest, and hopefully last, accident was caused by a woman who ran a yield sign, but whose husband ran around with a video camera and tried to blame it on me. I think majority rules here, don't you?

The saddest part about this chapter is that most of those men are married. Now, I can't imagine being married to a hot headed driver, since my husband drives like a little old lady. If you placed a huge straw hat with a cabbage rose on top, you wouldn't be able to tell them apart. I do not poke fun at him, because it was a man who, while drunk two times the legal limit, hit my husband head-on at fifty five miles per hour. Sadly, this man, who was married and had a small child, died. My husband suffered head injuries, knee injuries, and facial and mouth injuries. The lasting effects on my hubby were devastating, and even though this happened more than ten years ago, he still drives with fear. While we can joke all we want about getting lost, there is nothing funny about hot-headed or drunk drivers. They are extremely dangerous.

I am very protective of my car. The day I drove it off the dealership lot, I argued with the mechanic because I didn't want the gaudy dealership decal sticker on my back bumper. Men, on the other hand, love bumper stickers. Personally, I think they are ugly, most of them don't make any sense, and they deface the paint job on a car. However, some bumper stickers have given me a laugh or two.

My mother, who is this sweet-faced lady in her mid-sixties, was driving along and spotted a car with a bumper sticker. She got up close enough to read it, and caught the eye of the male driver, who was laughing hysterically and pointing at her. It soon became apparent to her why, when, shocked, she read: UNLESS YOU'RE A HEMORRHOID, GET OFF MY ASS! My husband threatened to buy a bumper sticker that said, IF YOU TAILGATE ME, I'LL FLICK A BOOGER ON YOUR WINDSHIELD! Or, having received several speeding tickets in my time, I like BAD COP! NO DONUT! Now, the hypocrisy of this sticker just can't be ignored: MEAN PEOPLE SUCK, on the bumper of a guy cutting people off and giving them the finger.

It is almost impossible to get from point to point without encountering a crazy male driver. For this problem I have no solution. All I could suggest is to laugh it off, since they really do look like idiots, as they scream, holler, and flip people off. As for their bumper stickers, I have no problems with them, as long as I am not forced to display one on my gorgeous car.

Chapter Nine

"I'm Sick! I Need More Kleenex! Where's My Soup? I'm Thirsty! Where's The Remote?"

I am fully convinced that it was a man who set the precedence for today's wedding vows. After all, what other sadistic moron would include the words "in sickness"? It had to be a man, that's all there is to it. Women's rights got rid of the part that stated we had to "obey" him (yeah right, in his dreams), so I am wondering what movement will outlaw the part that says we have to take care of them when they are sick.

Now, please don't get me wrong I really do like caring for sick people. I do! Really. I just hate having to listen to the moaning, groaning, and complaining that takes place when my mate is sick. Now, if only he would show the same compassion for me when I'm not feeling well, then I wouldn't mind as much. I do understand that he can't help it, but for the sake of my sanity, keep the whining to a minimum, will you? I mean honestly, I *know* you are sick, you don't need to keep moaning and repeating it over and over and over every fifteen seconds.

Case in point: When I was sick with the flu (yes, that's right, the same flu when he hid the toilet paper), he thought it was totally hilarious to watch me run as fast as I could into the bathroom to puke. He even went so far as to mimic the gagging noises and then ask me what I would like for dinner, namely, tuna casserole. Ugh! Then, when I was at the height of the flu and had it coming out both ends, I ran into the bathroom and couldn't decide if I should sit or stand. Tough choice, huh? I finally decided that I had to sit first, and yelled for my hubby to bring me something to puke in. Grinning from ear to ear, he grabbed the crusty, smelly baking pan that we had cooked fish in the night before. Since I was puking up the remainder of that lovely supper, the sight of that pan increased my nausea tenfold, and I screamed at him to take it away, take it away, and bring me something else to use, NOW! Still giggling, he returned a few seconds later with the orange juice pitcher. Good grief! Having no choice, I let loose, and later ended up throwing out the pitcher. Now, if that had been reversed and I had been the one giggling, he would have bawled like a baby, all the while blubbering, "*It's not funnnnnny! I'm sicccckkkk!*" And as for offering him a smelly old, crusted-up fish pan, he probably would've thrown it at me.

My good friend in Florida has a hubby who just disintegrates whenever she is sick. One night, weak after a gut-wrenching battle with the stomach flu, she curled up on the couch with her head in his lap, only to be rudely awakened a couple of hours later by being dumped on the floor. Apparently the big game was over and he wanted to go to bed, so instead of simply waking her up, he rolled her off him and tried to gently lower her to the floor. So in addition to the flu she also had bruises and rug burns on her hip from plopping onto the carpet.

I have come to the conclusion that a lot of men are useless in the face of their wives being sick. However, we are counted upon to wait on them hand and foot when they don't feel good. Where's *my* soup? I can't find *my* remote! I need more Kleenex! I don't feel good! Rub *my* back! In talking with friends and interviewing strangers, we all had one common denominator about sick hubbies: Send 'em off to the hospital until they fully recover.

Chapter Ten

Belly Laughs, Bad Jokes, And Other Public Embarrassments

I think one of the goals of early education should be to teach the male gender how to behave properly in a public place. Just ask any female who has had to suffer through some really bad jokes, loud, raucous laughter, and the myriad of other horrendous behaviors that, over time, have caused some major public embarrassments.

Men just don't get it, despite frantically whispered warnings by their spouse to tone it down. Among the most dangerous situations to be in publicly? A group of men together. In this situation, almost anything can, and usually does, happen. Forget that you are sitting at the dinner table, with your hands covering your face in mortification while he relates his latest tasteless and usually not very funny joke. Or how about when most of the other people at the table, in the finest restaurant in town, are sitting with their eyes glazed over, trying not to fall asleep, while your man (if you really want to claim him at that point) is boring them to tears with a detailed explanation of his latest high-tech laser disc player. Note the word *most* since all of the other males at the table are listening attentively to your man's long winded ramblings. This demonstrates that men really do know how to listen, they just choose not to when their wives are doing the talking. It's selective hearing at its finest. And how many times have you sent a silent prayer up to the powers that be, asking that this elegant dinner not turn into a discussion of revolting bodily functions, only to be ignored? In marriage, we, as women, send up a lot of silent prayers.

Almost always, when discussing this topic with my embarrassed female friends, the conversation begins with an indignant, "You are *not* going to believe what that...that...(sputter, sputter) unmannered, self-centered jerk did last night!" Many a cup of coffee has been shared while trying to calm down and convince a friend that, yes, he is a jerk, but no, you are not alone. All men behave this way.

My husband (he pops up a lot, doesn't he?) has a fondness for embarrassing me in the grocery store. He does this in many ways, the worst being the "Fart & Run," and the second worst is...well, to find out, keep on reading.

His favorite trick is to walk away while we are in the grocery store. He usually does this while I am looking in the opposite direction, talking in midsentence, which leaves me to walk around not realizing he has sneaked off somewhere else. I feel like such a dope, standing there talking to myself. Most of the time, the first indication I have that he is gone will be when some kind or bemused stranger will walk up and point out that nobody is listening. Talk about wanting to choke him. It also drives me up the wall when he wanders off, and I have to go and find him, almost like a parent would search for an unruly child. It gets worse when I have to have him paged, "Could Tim please report to the service desk! Your wife is looking for you!" Why do men have to put us through this?

My husband also tends to stumble over written words. This has led to some interesting situations, the most entertaining being the trip to the store when we bought a fax machine. Poor Tim, he had never seen the word *facsimile* in print before. Amused, he gestured to the salesclerk, and said, with a grin, "This looks like a nice face smile!" The funny part? He was totally serious.

My good friend Beth is blind (you'll meet her again in another chapter), and once at an alternative music concert, her husband, David, during a lull in the intermission, decided to state his opinion about the perfume that another nearby concert-goer was wearing. In a voice loud enough for everyone around us to hear, he asked "How come it smells like pesticide in here?" Earning nasty looks from the malodorous offender, Beth tried to keep her voice to an embarrassed whisper as she hissed, "That's *not* pesticide, it's patchouli oil!" Now, to better understand part of the embarrassment, patchouli oil was a favorite amongst the hippie generation, and there are striking similarities between today's alternative and the hippies of yesteryear. Beth, being a modern-day hippie, didn't want to offend anyone by stating this, but since I appreciate enlightenment, I just thought I'd toss it in.

Beth also likes The Grateful Dead, and David likes to blurt out in public whenever the subject comes up, "Yeah, he's gratefully dead!" He just doesn't seem to understand that, with regard to the Dead, that is the most overused saying around, even though David is specifically referring to Jerry Garcia. Yep, David is a bunch of laughs all right.

Another friend, Diane, was at a party with her husband, Don, at a very posh residence, when suddenly he had to use the bathroom. Unfortunately, he had to go number two, and it wasn't pretty. As she tells it, he finished his business and reached for the toilet paper, only to discover that there wasn't any left on the roll. In a panic, with his pants around his ankles, he frantically began opening drawers and cabinets, all the while thinking that surely there had to be a roll there somewhere. After he had examined all possible hiding places he opened one drawer, and unearthed, to his horror, a full bag of cotton balls. Diane just about convulses with laughter when she repeats what he said when he came out. "Have you ever tried to wipe your ass with a handful of cotton balls?" he whispered to her in embarrassment. Well, according to Diane, he did, and it was not a pleasant experience. In dismay, he finished the job as quickly as he could and watched wide-eyed as the cotton balls mushroomed to double their size when they hit the water. Then a new panic hit him as he chanted "Please don't let them clog the toilet! Please don't let them clog the toilet! Oh Pleeeaassse don't let them clog the toilet!" as the water swirled around and around, and thankfully went down without a problem. With his secret safe, he went out, told Diane what had happened, and, without much support from his giggling wife, tried to find a tactful way to let the hosts know that they needed to replenish the paper. As Diane put it, only Don would end up in such a predicament.

I told Diane not to worry, my husband went one better. One night at a party, he went around taking a poll. The subject you ask? He polled people to find out their wiping habits in the bathroom. He asked them if they were rollers, folders, or bunchers. Give me a break, will ya?

Tim, one night when we were talked into going roller skating with my nephews, some of their friends, and their parents, got a bad case of diarrhea. We giggled at his plight as he made a beeline for the bathroom. About twenty minutes later he hadn't returned to the floor, so we went searching for him. We found him sitting on a bench, looking forlorn. When asked what was wrong he replied, "There are no doors on the bathroom stalls!" Poor Tim had been trying to hold it. I guess it must have passed, since he returned to skating, but not five minutes later, he once again made a beeline for the rest room. His brother went to see if he was okay, and found him in the middle of a diarrhea attack, with little kids pointing, laughing, and yelling "What stinks in here?" I really did feel sorry for him at that point, but it was still rather embarrassing.

Now, to me, this is the ultimate embarrassment. I have a newly married friend. Her hubby is a surgeon, and he was doing a rotation out of town during the week, so they were only together on the weekends. One week, lonely for him, she drove down and spent the week at his apartment. When he came home for the weekend, in front of their friends, he proudly presented her with a handful of cardboard tubes. In horror and shock, she could feel this wave of red-hot embarrassment sweeping over her as she stared at him, while she waited for an explanation, and he waited for a response. "Some of your curlers fell into the trash when you were at the apartment last week," he said, pleased with himself. "I picked 'em all up and brought them back for you." As the other people in the room exploded with laughter, I tried to explain that no, these weren't curlers, they were *used tampon tubes*! All of a sudden, as the realization hit him, he looked down at his outstretched hand, which was still clutching the tubes, his eyes then glazed over, and he dropped the tubes as though he had been exposed to bubonic plague. This man is a doctor, and he didn't know what a tampon tube looked like! He beat a hasty retreat out of the room to go decontaminate. The friends, still hysterical with laughter, were by now doubled over, beating the furniture. And the doctor's wife was left standing in the middle of the room with the tampon tubes and her dignity on the floor scattered around her feet.

In all of these situations our men like to continue with their antics, until we either shut them up or remind them of the errors of their ways. Divorce court is also an option.

Chapter Eleven

Apple Meatloaf and Other Nauseating Attempts at Cooking (Recipes Included)

One night, dog tired from another hard day at work, I came home to a beautifully set dinner table, elegant tapered candles, and crystal wine goblets. The atmosphere was set for a perfect dinner. Or so I thought. Tim had really outdone himself this time, and I was impressed to say the least.

Beaming with pride, he set a plate down in front of me and, gingerly, with Tim watching me closely, I took a bite—then I gagged. I managed to swallow that nasty bite of food, took a huge sip of my drink, regained my composure, and tried nonchalantly to ask what it was. "Apple meatloaf," he replied, grinning. He was not kidding. After I examined it a bit further, I found that there were indeed chunks of apple and apple peel mixed in with the ground beef.

Upon quizzing him a bit further, I also discovered that he had added whole cloves (I think that's what I bit into that made me gag), cinnamon, and several other spices that were never intended to go with ground beef.

Then I almost died when he told me that since the recipe called for a large pan, he had baked this little, tiny, one pound loaf in, I kid you not, *the turkey roaster!* Not only had he *cooked* it in the turkey roaster, he had also *burned* it in the turkey roaster. Scorched, blackened, incinerated, however you want to describe it, half of it was stuck to the bottom of the pan. Evidently he had scraped the rest of it off and served it to me. Not wanting to hurt his feelings, since, after all, he did make the attempt, I tried as hard as I could to choke it down, but ended up spitting it out into the napkin when he wasn't looking. My dog was no help whatsoever. She turned up her nose, and for the first time in history, stopped begging at the table and went to lie down. Thanks a lot for the support, Heidi.

Now I know that any man reading this will manage to twist everything around by telling horror stories about his wife's cooking, and yes, my hubby has sat through some really unpalatable meals that I've prepared over the years. My first attempt at bean soup comes to mind, since the both of us, and the dog, had the runs for a couple of days. But at some point, common sense has to prevail. You just don't cook one pound of ground beef in a roasting pan big enough for a twenty pound turkey, and try as you might to disguise it, scorched food by candlelight is still scorched food. At least I knew when my cooking didn't turn out right, and I would have never dared serve it to anyone. Maybe his belief was that since I couldn't see it because of the dim lighting, I wouldn't know what I was eating. *Yeeeech!*

Just for laughs, I put a new spin on the art of bad cooking. Not only have I included the horror stories, I've also included the recipes. So ladies, put on your aprons, get out those turkey roasters—and antacid—and let's start cooking!

TIM'S APPLE MEATLOAF

Here's the infamous apple meatloaf. Guaranteed to gag a maggot. I was afraid to ask where he came up with this delightful (*not!*) recipe.

1 pound ground beef
1 large red apple, chopped, leaving seeds, peel and stem intact.
½ cup ketchup
1 teaspoon ground cinnamon
1 teaspoon whole cloves
1 teaspoon whole allspice
1 medium onion, chopped
1 clove garlic, pressed

½ cup bread crumbs
2 eggs

Equipment Needed: 1 large turkey roasting pan, no lid required.

Preheat oven to 450 degrees (higher temperatures make it cook faster). Mix ground beef, egg, bread crumbs, garlic, onion and spices together. (Make sure to use extra cinnamon, if you like the taste. After all, adding an extra spoonful will make the recipe taste that much better). Pat into a football shaped loaf and place in the ungreased turkey roaster. Bake approximately one and a half hours, or until the meatloaf is stuck to the bottom of the pan, charred black and smoking. A working smoke detector will help you tell when it's done. Remove from the turkey roaster by using a heavy duty spatula. Just keep scraping and prying until you work it loose. Turn the meatloaf upside down to remove any blackened portion that didn't get stuck to the bottom of the roasting pan. Garnish with half a bottle of ketchup and serve. Don't forget the antacid!

BOB'S CARL BUDDING BEEF AND VEGETABLES

(Kate, bless your heart, I promised I'd put it in, so here you go!)

Lisa M. Fuhs

When talking to my friend Kate in Iowa about bad hubby recipes, she doubles over. Partly in laughter, and partly in gastrointestinal agony, remembering the time she called home and asked her husband Bob to start dinner. She had a package of frozen vegetables, the kind used for stir fry, complete with sauce, you just had to add the beef. She explained in detail just how to whip up this very simple dish and, satisfied that he understood (wrong), hung up the phone.

Upon arriving home, she walked in the door, and noticed this foul, kind of smoky odor coming from the kitchen. Alarmed, she raced in and found that Bob had indeed finished making supper. The problem? He was too lazy to thaw the beef needed for this dish, so he went to the freezer and defrosted several packages of Carl Budding beef lunch meat, chopped it up and added it to the veggies. Needless to say, it was less than edible. The dogs, on the other hand, loved the Carl Budding stir fry and gobbled it down. They paid for it later, when they got a severe case of diarrhea. I'm not sure, but I think Kate ended up ordering a pizza. For you sadistic, brave souls who love a good case of the trots, here's the recipe:

1 package stir fry vegetables & sauce
6 packages Carl Budding lunch meat, chopped in bite-size pieces.

Gently saute the veggies and add enough liquid to create a sauce. Then add the bite-size pieces of Carl Budding beef. Serve to those who will eat it, namely the dogs.

MASHED POTATO GLUE

This recipe was contributed anonymously by a friend, whose husband is one of those he-man types who loves a good competition. In this case, he was competing with his wife to see who could get their portion of the dinner preparations done faster. Here are the ingredients:

4 medium potatoes, peeled
¼ cup milk
2 tablespoons butter
1 tablespoon fresh parsley, chopped
Salt and pepper to taste

Wash and peel potatoes. Fill a large saucepan with water and bring to a boil. Cook potatoes until tender. Drain.

Mash potatoes, and add the rest of the ingredients. If the potatoes are still lumpy, continue to beat vigorously with all of your strength, until potatoes are shiny and glue-like in texture.

This recipe works especially well for men, since they have the upper body strength to beat the potatoes into just the right, sticky, shiny, gluey consistency. *Ick!*

AFTERSHAVE SANDWICHES

Okay, this is another one from the Tim Hall of Fame. I was working overtime at my job one year, and, since I did not have enough time to prepare my lunch, hubby decided to be "helpful" and make it for me. What a sweetie! I went to work with a beautiful sandwich, fruit, and yogurt, and all morning long thought about how lucky I was to have such a caring husband. Then it was time for lunch. I opened my sandwich, and, smiling happily, took a bite. Big mistake. It was like biting into a bottle of aftershave. Apparently he hadn't washed his hands after applying his aftershave, and then touched my bread. I had to spit out my sandwich, and ended up eating the yogurt and fruit instead. Here's the recipe:

2 slices bread
butter
Turkey breast
Lettuce & tomato
Aftershave

Put on a heavy dose of aftershave, and make sure you don't wash your hands afterward. This will ensure that the fragrance is successfully transferred to the bread. After you prepare the sandwich, place in a plastic bag and allow to sit, refrigerated, for approximately four hours. This will allow the various flavors to "blend." Be certain that this is the sandwich you put in your spouse's lunch, as you really wouldn't want to eat it yourself!

RICHARD'S WEEKLY MENU

My father had three gourmet dishes that he expertly prepared for us kids whenever my mother would work. From him we learned to appreciate chef de haut cuisine.

Monday
Hotdogs
Buns
Choice of condiments
Boil the hotdogs until done. Place in buns, and serve.

Tuesday
Sliced American cheese
White bread
Butter
Heat butter in a large skillet, place cheese between bread slices, and fry until cheese is melted.

Wednesday
Canned ravioli
Open the can of ravioli, pour into saucepan, heat and serve.

Thursday
See menu for Monday.

Friday
See menu for Tuesday.

Saturday
See menu for Wednesday.

Sunday
Thank goodness Mom's home!

BILL'S BEANS ON BREAD

My father was a mediocre cook, and one of his favorite meals was baked beans on toast. One night, the toaster gave out and he served my sister baked beans on plain white bread. She pitched a fit, called me up and told me that he was trying to make her eat beans on bread. *Ick.* Needless to say, I picked her up and took her out for dinner. My father, deciding to sulk, stayed home and ate his beans on bread.

1 can baked beans

Plain white bread

Cook the beans until hot, pour over the bread and serve.

AL'S MICROWAVE CHICKEN PATTIES

Al will probably remain single forever, and part of the reason is his lack of culinary skills. One day he invited my friend Sarah over for dinner at his apartment. Here this poor girl probably thought she had hooked a real prize until he grabbed a package of frozen breaded chicken patties, and proceeded to pop them in the microwave. Now, most intelligent people know that some foods just cannot be cooked in a microwave, since they tend to harden, or the breading becomes soggy. Al, being the brain-child he was, cooked Sarah's chicken until it was rock hard, and virtually inedible.

1 package frozen breaded chicken patties
Buns
1 microwave
1 chisel
1 date you do not intend to see a second time

First, invite your date over for dinner. Buy frozen chicken patties so you are sure to let her know just how cheap a date you really are. Next, to effectively scare her off, microwave the patties until they are as hard as a rock. Serve them along with a chisel so that she doesn't chip a tooth trying to bite them. Then stand back so that she can beat a hasty retreat home. One footnote: It is probably not a good idea to try and call her again.

This was just a sampling of the unappetizing dishes prepared by our galloping gourmets. Galloping because that's exactly what we end up doing in order to reach the bathroom as fast as we can. If you are fortunate enough to have married a professional chef, you really don't know how lucky you've got it.

Chapter Twelve

Hey Honey, Listen! I Can Burp The Alphabet!

One night, feeling a little romantic, I prepared this elegant, seductive dinner for myself and my husband. He came home from work to candlelight, soft music, fresh flowers, and an incredibly delicious meal of lobster and shrimp. The cherry on the whole evening was that I served it in a skimpy lace teddy and four inch spiked heels. I was really cookin' in more ways than one.

Well, Mr. Manners managed to behave himself for about ten minutes (a world record for him), and I foolishly thought that this evening might actually show some promise. There we sat, looking enticingly at each other, toasting the evening with champagne in crystal goblets. Anticipating the events to come, we somehow managed to finish our food.

As we got up, he let loose with the loudest,

most disgusting belch I've ever heard (think Booger in *Revenge Of The Nerds*). This was followed by a hearty, "Great dinner, hon!" and a beaming smile from my Prince Charming. Prince Disgusting would be a better term for him. Okay, so far the night wasn't totally ruined, but oh wait! One belch led to two, and two to three and so on and so forth. You get the picture. Each bringing gales of laughter from my beloved.

Ugh! There's nothing like trying to cozy up to a man who continues to belch garlic shrimp in your face. Needless to say, I went to bed alone, furious that all of my efforts had once again gone unappreciated. His garbled explanation of how belching is supposed to be a compliment to the cook in some other countries fell on deaf ears. Was it too much to ask that he at least "pretend" that he had some manners just for one night?

Okay, I *do* understand that burping is a natural bodily function, and that sometimes you really can't control it, but you *can* excuse yourself to avoid grossing out the people around you.

Burping is right up there with farting in the male "I can't help it, it's too funny to behave myself" category. Men simply can't resist an opportunity to show just how manly they are. What's the second most popular mark of manhood? Being able to out-burp, out-gas, out-spit, and out-hack any other male within braying distance. Yuck!

My brother-in-law Dave (yes the guy of the Pull-my-finger fame) is also an expert at burps. To an eleven-year-old, being able to belch out "Yabba-dabba Doo!" by a guy who looked just like Fred Flintstone was pretty cool stuff. I used to ask Dave to demonstrate his talents for my friends. Then I grew up and got a fiancée of my own. Guess what? Then it wasn't quite so funny anymore.

Thank goodness that there are only two really loathsome bodily functions for our men to embarrass us with. At least only two that make noise. Unless you count his mouth, which can usually make plenty of noise.

Just writing this chapter made me queasy at times. Some of these burps defy explanation, and as for funny, well that depends on whether you're male or female. Take a wild guess as to which gender will think it's funny? I have managed to identify through experience over the years the many different types of burps:

The Silent but Deadly Garlic Burp. Guaranteed to stimulate the gag reflex of everyone within a ten foot radius. You can always identify the culprit by the way he is doubled over, giggling at everyone's discomfort.

The Booger Burp. Named after one of the characters in the movie *Revenge Of The Nerds*. The aim of this burp is to demonstrate for all who don't want to hear just how loud and long a man can hold a burp. The sound alone is enough to make one blow chunks. These are the type of burps that get the testosterone in males going, and starts those nasty frat party competitions, where they are cheering, and chugging carbonated beverages, trying to out-belch one another. A word of advice: Once it reaches this point, you can't fight it, and it's better to leave the men alone to act like little boys.

The Burp & Blow. Now to me, this is the lowest form of burping, but very popular among our guys. This is when he burps and blows it in your face. To those of you who have had to sit through this, you know just how sick it is. My advice would be to blow it right back at him.

The Alphabet Burp. Now, even I will admit that these can be funny, if done under the right circumstances. These are when he belches out words, or if he's really talented, complete sentences. The sky's the limit with this type of burp.

The Juicy Burp. Now these are absolutely

disgusting. This is a kind of hack/belch, usually ending with a huge, loud, moist hack, followed by spitting up a big old yucky, yellow hocker. It's enough to make you shudder, as you look on with distaste. *Ick!*

The Straight-From-The-Stomach Burp. This can be silent or loud, but the one common factor here is stench. These are burps created from the depths of his stomach, guaranteed to give you a whiff of everything he has eaten for the past two days. If you see one of these coming, run, don't walk, in the opposite direction.

The Rotten Egg Burp. Now these defy description. Sulfur-based, they are the worst of the burps as far as pungency is concerned. Not only do they smell horrendous, they linger too. I have yet to figure out what foods cause these burps, and I can only be grateful that they don't happen very often. A couple of times a year, at most. When they do occur, they last for days, and you literally have to open all doors and windows to get the awful smell out of your house. Whew! They are bad.

The Beer/Brat/Onion Burp. This burp usually happens after a cookout, monster truck rally, or any other outdoor, male-type of event. It's really attractive when he gets home, all dusty, dirty, and smelly, and wants to get romantic. At that point, it's time for you to take your pillow and blanket out on the couch. My suggestion? Next time, you leave him home, and you down the beer, brats and onions, then come home and cozy up to him, while belching this putrid stench in his face. Romantic? I think not.

The Talking Burp. This is when he is talking and accidentally belches midsentence. While this is not preventable, most guys usually just burp and keep on talking. Not an "excuse me" in sight. I knew a Korean guy who would eat Katechee (fermented cabbage and garlic), and then proceed to belch out every other word. Not a pleasant experience at all!

The Bogus Burp. This is when he burps without having to, just to be obnoxious. My husband has a bad habit of doing this when I am trying to talk to him about something he doesn't want to talk about. "Bbbllllaaapppp! Sorry dear. Now what was it you were saying?" It's enough to make me climb the walls. If your guy does this, just keep on repeating yourself. He will either keep forcing belches until he pukes, or give up and actually listen to what you are trying to say.

Last, but not least: (Yes, I know this is more than ten, but I couldn't help myself!)

The Near-Puke Burp. These are when he burps and almost pukes. Mostly it's just the burper who suffers, but there are those guys who delight in telling everyone around just how bad the burp tasted. They take great pleasure in describing how they can feel the chunks of food, still identifiable, sloshing around in their throats, except now it's all mixed up with a sour liquid, and could almost qualify as puke. They have an uncontrollable need, if you missed the actual event, to make sure they repeat every rancid, curdled, nauseating moment. Now, if you'll excuse me, I think I'll go throw up.

Those are the ten (okay, eleven) top burps. Gross? You bet. Funny? Well, sometimes. But for the most part, it's really pretty disgusting, and almost always done during inopportune times. Hopefully, you will be one of the minority of wives whose hubbies have some manners, but more than likely you recognized someone you love, but don't want to claim, when you read this chapter.

Chapter Thirteen

Creative Uses For A Man In A Reclining Chair

Ahh the sight of a snoring man sacked out in a reclining chair! It's enough to warm your heart when you see your beloved sleeping peacefully, with the remote clutched possessively in one hand, while the other hand wipes away the drool as it trickles down his chin and splashes onto the front of his three-day-old spotted T-shirt. Warms your heart, that is, as your blood does a slow boil.

La-Z-Boy is a company I loath. Just the name is enough to spark feelings of rage in most wives. After all, just how much more lazy can a person get, snoring away while their overwhelmed wife does all the housework? I guess if it weren't this company it would be some other company creating these oh-so-comfy chairs that are the nemesis of any marriage.

Today these seats have ceased being simple, basic chairs that recline, they are also computerized, with more amenities than a luxury car. Take for instance these new recliners that massage your back and feet and have the remote control built right into the arm, along with the one hundred CD changer, and at the push of a button, a holograph of a tall blond French maid appears to cater to his ego: "Oh Georgie, I just *love* your three-day-old stubble!" Gush! Gush! "Your t-shirt looks *so* attractive, with all those old food spots on it!" Gush! Gush! "And those drool stains! Oh, what a turn on!" Gush! Gush! "How about another beer to make that adorable little potbelly bigger?" It's sickening. At least it's not real. Not yet anyway, but it won't be long before those damned chairs will completely eliminate the need for a wife.

Now that I think about it, let technology rule! The quicker the better.

For those of you who are fed up with that annoying, immovable lump in the recliner blocking out the view of your beautifully decorated living room, I have come up with some creative uses for your lazy man and his La-Z-Boy:

An art-deco plant hanger. Note, his pot belly makes the perfect spot to place that hibiscus.

A deterrent for would-be burglars. You've heard of the blow up man? Well, you've already got a live one. A note of caution: Some men may not wake up in the event of a real burglary, therefore you might want to also have a large, mean dog on the premises.

A climbing post for a declawed cat. God forbid a cat with claws should try to climb up on him, it might actually wake him up.

A giant doorstop.

Step stool for reaching high places.

Oversized floor lamp. Drool is an excellent conductor of electricity.

Medical research test subject, to test the correlation between prolonged television exposure and catatonia.

A model for the poster hubby, advocating the benefits of staying single.

Extra table space for folding laundry.

Snack table for when you have your friends over. He can also double as an interesting conversation piece.

Just a short footnote to this chapter: I sold my hubby's recliner at our last garage sale, for seventy-five bucks, no less. Although I was overjoyed to be rid of it, I did experience a fleeting pang of a guilty conscience for the young wife who bought it for her new hubby. Wow! Did she have a lot to learn or what? Needless to say, the guilt passed, and I went shopping. Who says I couldn't have the last laugh?

Chapter Fourteen

The Culturally Disabled Man

My attempts to bring my husband into the grown-up world of classical music, fine wines, and elegant dinners at five-star restaurants have all but been a disaster to date, anyhow. He just doesn't get it. At an elegant restaurant, all he does is gripe about the prices and complain about the size of the portions. After all, how can you be expected to fill up when you aren't at the local greasy spoon on all you can eat night??? To top it off, while at the dinner table in a fancy Chinese restaurant, he once blew his nose into the fine linen napkin. Mortified, I happened to glance over at the waiter, who had witnessed the entire nauseating episode. He stood there shaking his head in dismay, while offering me looks of pity. "*Tsk, tsk*" he seemed to say, "That guy is worse than the one we had in here last night!" I was then further embarrassed upon leaving when the

Chinese waiter babbled something in his native tongue to the other waiter, while gingerly picking up the napkin with two fingers and pulling a sour face.

Gourmet to my husband means extra cheese on his bean burrito at the local Taco Bell. Good manners means he promises he won't fart until we're clear of the restaurant. Classical music means early rock bands from years past, with opera reminding him of some poor lady screaming in pain while being jabbed in the rear with a pin. Ballroom dancing is out of the question, as he never quite got over his break dancing phase of fifteen years ago, and during our one and only excursion to an art gallery, he made a nice, loud, obnoxious comment on the size of the hooters of the woman in one of the pricey paintings.

I have all but given up.

At some point during our marriages, we must face the reality that most men do not appreciate nor understand the value of adding culture to our lives.

The following is a list of the top cultural faux pas that our men make:

Opera. The name of that talk-show host.

Fine wines. The three dollar bottle of wine purchased at the gas station on his way home.

Play. Something exciting to watch on Monday Night Football.

Bach. The sound a really great burp makes.
Classical. Vintage autos, Led Zeppelin.
Formal dress. The jeans he didn't wear to fix the car.
Good manners. Not using his hands.
Gourmet. Pizza with extra toppings, and beer in a glass instead of a bottle.
Social events. Tractor pulls, monster truck rallies.
Art. A portrait of Elvis painted on a black velvet canvas that was purchased at the corner gas station.
Table manners. Using a napkin instead of his sleeve.
Visiting etiquette. Remembering to put the toilet seat back down versus leaving it up.

Sadly, there is a growing population of culturally disabled men in the world today. As a wife, I will continue my fruitless efforts to educate, painful as it may be. I believe in the necessity of adding a touch of class and culture to one's life. Now if only I could figure out how to get him to cooperate.

Chapter Fifteen

Cheap, Cheap, CHEAP!

Forever emblazoned upon my weary brain is the memory of my first year of marriage, when my new husband came rushing in to tell me he had learned of double coupon day at the local Pick 'n Save grocery store. On a limited budget, he was trying to save us some money, bless his frugal little heart, so he gathered up a bunch of coupons and set off eagerly for the store.

He returned an hour later, with, I kid you not, and I'll swear to this on anyone's mother's grave, since I do not have any pictures to prove it, *thirty-three boxes of cereal.* Ugh. Proud as a peacock, he strutted into the living room and couldn't wait to show me just how cheap the cereal was. "Look honey! This one was only fifty cents!" he said, beaming. My husband beams a lot, if you haven't noticed. With the bile rising in my throat, and not wanting to show my dismay and distaste at having to eat cereal for the rest of my natural life, I managed a half-hearted smile, gave him a peck on the cheek, and told him he did a great job at saving us some money. I had to find something positive in this, you do understand.

The next few months were spent in culinary hell. We ate cereal constantly. Breakfast. Lunch. Dinner. Snacks. We had a cereal for every occasion, including special ones. In addition, we had a minuscule, one bedroom apartment, with a pocket-size kitchen, and no storage space worth mentioning. We had cereal boxes stacked everywhere: On the fridge, in every closet, under the bed, if there was a space for a cereal box, we found it. If there wasn't, we found one anyway. I even had to put up with boxes dropping onto my head when I would open the refrigerator door. I will, occasionally, still unconsciously duck when I open the fridge door. Even now, years later, I have to force myself to eat cereal. Cap'n Crunch makes me want to blow chunks.

Tim inherited his "thriftiness" from his grandfather. *Thriftiness* may not be the best word, but it is the kindest. I can think of several better words to describe him, but since he will probably end up reading this book, I don't think it would be appropriate to use them, unless I file for divorce first. To give you an idea of where this came from, Tim's grandfather, Tony, was probably the cheapest person around, next to

Tim, of course. He hated to spend a dime. He would buy a frozen pizza, then cut it into bite-size pieces, and then bake a couple of them at a time as a treat for visitors, namely us. It gets worse. He would wear clothes from many years past, and wouldn't throw them away for any amount of money, no matter what condition they were in. I distinctly remember one day when we went to visit, and found Grandma extremely irritated. When we quizzed her, she pointed to the back of Grandpa's shirt, and as we were gaping at it, related the events of the past few hours.

Apparently Tony had ripped the back of a threadbare, flannel shirt that he had had for years. I am talking *at least* two decades. This was his favorite shirt, and in many places you could see right through it. When Grandma went to wash it, she noticed that it had (*gulp*) fallen apart, ripping right down the back. She threw it away without saying anything to Grandpa, hoping he wouldn't notice. Well, when he took the garbage out, he noticed that his all-time favorite shirt was among the refuse, and he pitched a fit. Yelling at the top of his lungs, he demanded that she sew it up. Equally irked at the thought of being seen in public with Grandpa and his "shirt," she refused. This escalated into a huge battle, with Grandpa finally stomping off. He returned an hour or so later, wearing the shirt. Poor

Grandma almost had a stroke when he turned around to show off his "sewing" job. He had gotten into her sewing kit, and, using black thread, had stitched the entire backside of the shirt back together. I am talking gigantic, jet-black stitches, at least two inches long. From that day on he insisted on wearing that shirt every chance he could. "*It's a perfectly good shirt!*" He would shout whenever Grandma would protest. Things got so bad that eventually she stopped going out in public with him whenever he would wear his prize shirt. With genes like this, do you now understand what I am up against in my marriage?

This isn't the first time my husband has exhibited symptoms of his grandfather's "thriftiness." I hate the reduced bins at the grocery store almost as much as I hate cereal. The problem really has nothing to do with the fact that some people will think I am a die-hard snob who refuses to buy the dented and damaged goods. No that's not it at all. It really has a lot more to do with the way my husband acts every time we happen upon one. His eyes grow big; his breathing becomes faster; his pupils become dilated; and he gets all excited, like a kid with a handful of pennies in a candy store. I practically have to fasten a rope around his waist to keep him from falling in. He digs and searches until he has examined every item in the bin. It is most embarrassing. I'll usually give a couple of tugs at his sleeve, fiercely whisper a few warnings about the dangers of getting stuck headfirst in the bin, threaten him with divorce, and then give up and slink away, hoping nobody saw us together. He will re-emerge an hour or so later, loaded down with reduced items, once again beaming, because he saved us some money. The strange looks we get at the checkout lanes are probably from those people who happened to walk by and see him bent over, his butt stuck up in the air, searching for bargains.

My husband also loves one-dollar bills, and he also loves to save his change in my kitchen canisters. You know, the ones that are meant for sugar, flour and noodles. Now this isn't such a bad habit, not bad at all, most of you are probably thinking, and you would be right—if not for those times when I am running short of cash and need gas in my car, only to find that the only currency in the house is quarters. Now, we are a professional couple in our mid-thirties, who own our own business. Do you have any idea how humiliating it is to drag along a bag full of quarters to pay for my gas? There are days that I feel like I'm in high school again and scrounging for change. Honestly, does he have to convert everything to coins? In his case, it's a resounding yes.

One dollar bills are worse. Instead of saving that twenty dollar bill, he will use it to purchase a candy bar, just to get the one dollar bills. It's deceiving, since he usually winds up with a stack of bills, but really only has about twenty dollars in his wallet. It drives me nuts. Period.

Now, I realize that Tim's cheapness is just a way of looking out for our finances. I really do appreciate all of the effort that goes into saving a dime here and there. One really sweet example of this would be when we were in college (as a matter of fact I think it was the same year that he bought all that cereal) and didn't have much money. I had to walk quite a distance in the winter to my classes and couldn't afford a back-pack. At Christmas that year, I unwrapped my present only to find a gorgeous, royal blue back-pack, complete with all of the pockets and hiding places. I was so excited! I reached over and gave him a huge hug, then proceeded to explore my gift. My excitement turned to dismay and then to laughter when I turned it over and found the words *Purina Dog Chow* emblazoned in gigantic letters on the back. I looked quizzically at Tim, who then told me that he had been saving the weight circles from the dog food bags until he had enough to send in for my backpack. Realizing that he had done this so that I could walk to my classes in comfort, I then cried. Since then I have tried (very hard in some cases) to be more appreciative of his efforts.

I guess I can, once again, consider myself

lucky. I have several dubious friends, of whom Grandpa would be proud. J.T. comes to mind. J.T. is an exceptionally intelligent individual, having several degrees in mathematics. However, what J.T. lacks are social skills. I mean he *really* lacks social skills. For instance, he had been dating Tammy for several months, and at a flea market J.T. saw a pretty, five-dollar ring at one of the booths. He bought it and gave it to Tammy. When poor, clueless Tammy got home, she excitedly told her mother, "Look, Mom! J.T. gave me a going-together ring!" Only to be corrected by J.T., who reached over and slipped the cheap ring off her finger, stating emphatically, "This is your engagement ring, and I will give it to you when we get engaged!" Needless to say, that ended the relationship right then and there. Another example of J.T.'s lack of social skills occurred when we had gone to a convenience store, and he bought me a candy bar. I said I would pay him back for it soon. The following week he called me at midnight, only to say, "I just happened to be in the neighborhood. Do you have the fifty-three cents you still owe me?" Good grief! Fifty-three cents! Needless to say, I hung up on him. Never a lender nor a borrower be. Especially when dealing with a genius without social skills.

Now, I know I don't speak for all men. Some really are generous to a fault. I am just speaking from my personal run-in's with my own versions of Scrooge. If a penny saved is a penny earned is your hubby's motto, you have my sympathies. If he loves to pinch pennies, maybe giving him a good pinch will wake him up. Who knows, it's worth a try.

Chapter Sixteen

Gadgets, Stereos, And Other Incredibly Boring Toys

My older sister Denise (yes, the one married to Dave, a/k/a Fred Flintstone, of the yabba-dabba doo, and pull-my-finger fame) is also a victim of modern technology. Dave's second love, next to my beautiful, intelligent sister and their two boys, is anything that has buttons, dials, a motor, or a remote control. This leaves his options wide open, and hers, well, that's a whole other story.

One night I arrived for a visit at her house and wanted to listen to one of her CDs. She shot me this skeptical look and proceeded to lead me into their theater room. Uncertain and more than a little alarmed by the way she was stomping, I reluctantly followed her.

Their entertainment room is impressive. I am talking big-screen television, as big as a set of double closet doors, tuner, high-tech stereo system that has speakers hooked up throughout the house, a separate security camera poised over the front door for the express purpose of, I kid you not, my brother-in-law Dave being able to see the pizza delivery man. A laser disc player; movie theater popcorn machine; remote-control lights; and, my sister's nemesis, the dreaded one-hundred-disc CD changer.

Pointing in vexation at the CD changer, she replied grimly, "It's in *there!* All my CDs disappear in *there*, and I never see them again!" She tried in vain to get the remote (one of about six) to work so we could listen to the CD, all to no avail. Lights kept flashing, Tina Turner kept blaring upstairs, and the television kept turning on and off.

Finally, doubled over with laughter, and partly out of pity for her, I told her to skip it. Keep in mind that this woman is a certified public accountant, no slouch by anyone's standards, but she was whipped by that system. And I am fairly sure at that point she would have liked to whip her husband too.

My hubby also loves gadgets. I absolutely, positively, unequivocally hate, abhor, and loath being stuck in an electronics store with him. It's so incredibly boring to just *stand* there, while he tediously adjusts the volume on a boom box, for forty-five solid minutes. Then he moves on to the tuner, the CD player, the equalizer. Yawn! You get the picture. Looking around, I see all of the other very bored gals, rolling their eyes and sighing, all while tapping their foot impatiently and waiting for their guys to finish fiddling.

Computer stores are even worse. Normal, everyday macho guys turn into computer geeks. They exchange their contact lenses for horn-rimmed, Coke-bottle thick glasses, button-down shirts, with the top button done up, and the ever-present pocket protectors when they enter a computer store. Tons of money, which could be better spent on me, is wasted on the latest 3-D game. I have yet to figure out the attraction. After all, what hubby doesn't want his wife to buy the latest red-hot fashions so she can look absolutely stunning when he takes her out for a night on the town, and at the most expensive five-star restaurant around? Don't you agree that this would be a much better way to blow several hundred dollars? I do. But no, he prefers to blow the dough, then sit for days on end, alone, staring at his screen, and listening to me (or better yet, tuning me out) complaining about his other "girlfriend"—the computer. I would be jealous, but I know "she" doesn't look nearly as good as I do in a black leather teddy. If he only knew what he was missing. Have you ever noticed that for men any and all inanimate objects are female?

When it comes to electronic and computer stores, I decided to wise up after the first year or two of marriage. Now, I do one of two things, either refuse to go into those stores with him, or if I do get stuck, he gets to go with me while I pick out something equally boring, like crafts, nail polish or makeup. My motto is: Don't get mad, get even.

Personally, I admire his skill in learning what every button on the remote control is for, and how to program it. I just don't have any desire to study the manuals for hours on end, as if I am studying madly for a big final exam in college. I have better things to do with my limited time.

I also think men look really asinine, all clustered together, going gaga over all that electronic/computer stuff. Doesn't it remind you of the old joke, "How many people does it take to change a light bulb?" Change it to, "How many men does it take to figure out the remote?" and it might actually be funny. My friend Beth's husband spends more time with the computer in a week than he does with her.

Boys will be boys, and our little boys must play. The best we can do is try and stay out of their way, and make sure our CDs don't get lost in the mayhem of gadgets that take over every room in the house.

Here is a list of our little boys and their toys:

Big wheels vs. Four big wheels
Tonka Truck vs. Monster truck
Toy telephone vs. Cellular phone

Lisa M. Fuhs

Snow sled vs. Snowmobile for a sled

Fisher Price Tape Recorder/Player vs. State-of-the-art stereo system with fifty remote controls, CD player capable of reading your mind to know what song you want next, a tuner that actually can pick up signals from life on other planets, an equalizer that is capable of enhancing the sounds of life on other planets. Okay, by now you must know that I'm kidding, but you get the idea.

Toy airplanes vs. Real airplanes

Board games vs. 3-D Computer games that cost seventy dollars each

Charlotte's Web vs. Web sites

Model kits vs. Models in skin magazines

Matchbox cars vs. Fully loaded sports cars with monthly payments that would blow your mind

I get so sick and tired of standing around waiting for my husband to play with every gadget he comes across. Programming the remote is an hour-long task, purchasing a new sound system is almost intolerable when he's around, and as for electronics in general, I am to the point where I refuse to participate in it. You can't beat 'em, so you might as while beat it and go shopping. I have come to realize that boys love their toys. Unfortunately, as men they still love their toys, they just cost a whole lot more.

Chapter Seventeen

Baby, You've Got No Style!

My first clue that my husband was clueless about decorating came about a week after we were married. Granted, we had lived together for a couple of years, but I honestly thought the "Damn, I'm good" mirror, the giant whisky bottle he kept his change in, along with the break-dancing posters were just left overs from his wild teen years. Never dreaming I would have to live with these hideous relics, literally, 'til death do us part, I set out, after our honeymoon, to tackle the impossible task of redecorating our apartment.

First, we went shopping for artwork. Not the expensive kind one would find in an art gallery, mind you, we were on a strict budget, but more like the kind you'd find at Sears. I immediately locked eyes on a gorgeous floral print, and he excitedly pointed to the most horrifically ugly, garish, huge, gold-colored etching of a sailing ship. One probably could have used it as a mirror. Shiny, completely gold, right down to the frame, and blinding bright enough to burn holes in the walls when the morning sunlight reflected off it, it was love at first sight for my hubby. Wanting to please him, I cringed inwardly while the salesclerk rang up our purchase. This lovely print went front and center in the middle of our living room, right next to the tarnished antique replica of the town bank which, (surprise) was actually a piggy bank that he had found in the garbage, and the hideous nautical temperature gage with three dials that he insisted we hang right next to the gaudy sailing ship picture. Are you starting to picture the "theme" of our home yet? Anchors away! So much for the Waterford crystal candy dishes, floral arrangements, and antique linens and lace. I vowed right then and there to find a way to sink his ship.

Now, years later, I realize that I had it far better in the decorating department than many new wives since my best friend got stuck with all of her hubby's hunting trophies hanging grotesquely in their living room. She is against the killing of animals of any kind, and gets a major case of the creeps when she has to walk into this room in the dark, only to feel as though the accusing, unmoving eyeballs of all of those dead animals are watching her.

Another friend (and this is even more embarrassing for me to write about) has a husband who, though in his mid-thirties, still spends hours painting his beloved pewter *Star Trek* and *Star Wars* action figures. Everywhere you can rest your eyes, you will find Spock, Captain Kirk, Data, Picard, R2D2 and Princess Leah. Waterford crystal? Hmmm...place it right next to the genuine replica of the Starship Enterprise phone please! Since she is blind, she really doesn't know how awful it looks, and all I can say is that in this case, her blindness is a blessing.

Another friend of mine, poor thing, had to live with her husband's fake, giant bug collection all over her home. From the outside to the inside there were fist-size butterflies, flies, crickets, and spiders jumping out from all of the plants and hidden corners. I felt crawly for weeks after visiting her.

Over the years I have slowly transformed my home into a place to be proud of. The gaudy gold picture has a new home in the garage, along with the giant whisky bottle and the nautical gauge. My attempts to redecorate were gradual at first, but over time they gained more and more acceptance and, I hope, liking by my husband.

I know we shouldn't be too hard on men who have no sense of style; after all, statistics show that most men in the decorating profession are gay. Therefore they wouldn't be married, but they probably have fabulously decorated homes. Big tough guys on the other hand seem to want to prove their sexuality by desecrating their homes with beer-can collections, football memorabilia, and the latest *Sports Illustrated* swimsuit model pictures. Flowers, art, and fancy china and crystal just aren't manly enough for these guys. It's almost as if they are trying to prove themselves with bad taste. I have found, if you can afford it, hire a decorator to redo your home, preferably one that's gay. They have incredible taste.

Take heart ye who are newly married! As the saying goes, This too shall pass. I just wonder if that person ever had to live with a giant bug collection?

Chapter Eighteen

Why I Hate the Home "Improvement" Store!

Maybe *hate* is too strong a word to use here. Perhaps dislike, despise, resent, or detest would be a better choice. I'm not sure where such strong feelings came from. I suspect that it might possibly have had a little something to do with the fact that every spare dollar is being spent on useless tools; car parts he will never use; or some project that, after he has spent a year's salary to buy, never leaves the safety of his head. If he actually does get around to starting the project, one of two things will usually happen: First, it will never be completed, or second, should it be completed, it's usually butt-ugly, dangerous or completely impractical.

Take my poor sister, yes, yes, I know, the one married to the master of the gassers, with the electronically booby-trapped house. She and her hubby struggled for almost ten years to complete the renovations on her home. When they finally could afford to redo the kitchen, she excitedly went and chose her dream cabinets. They were absolutely gorgeous. Solid cherry wood, with enough space to hide a dozen small children. Unfortunately, the brief glimpse in the showroom was all she had, because, for the next year, she had a lovely view of the packing boxes that the cabinets came in. There they sat, gathering dust, right smack in the middle of the dining room, while her hubby began and abandoned a host of other projects. *Arrrrrgggghhhhh*!

I remember going through the Sunday paper, only to find an ad for a do-it-yourself house. Two-thousand square feet, three bedrooms, two bathrooms, kitchen, dining room, family room. It sounded wonderful. Then sheer terror set in when I realized that, should my hubby see this, it would end up on our front lawn as the next big "project" he would tackle. Frantically searching my brain for a way to make this ad disappear, I wondered if he would be bright enough to notice a page or two missing…Pages 10, 11, 14, 15, 16 and so on. It wasn't a separate flyer, it was smack in the middle of the sports section. Great. It must have been a man who came up with this brainchild of wanting to place a home "improvement" ad in the most popular section known to guys.

It's gotten better and worse. Most of these ads are separate flyers. Better since I can go through the paper first and take out the flyers. Now, I always offer, sweetly of course, to go and get the Sunday paper. Worse if he beats me to the punch. Now, you might think it's a super advertising ploy, but the innovator behind this separate flyer scheme was a group of wives who were fed up with their second home being any and all home improvement stores. Pretty clever, huh?

My mother complains incessantly about the huge barn-like storage structure that my father, God rest his soul, put up a few years before he died. Now this was a man who continually had to have one or more useless projects going at the same time. In the case of the barn, it is two stories high, dirt brown, and blocks out my mother's view of the park behind her house. It didn't matter that her house is a simple ranch home on a standard size lot. He insisted on putting up that monstrosity, come what may.

My sister and I have also had the speaker cabinet wars. Back in the sixties, my father built two enormous, solid walnut speaker cabinets. They stand about four feet high, are very wide, colossal in size, and corner-shaped, so you must have two available corners to put them in. Lucky for me she has an enormous old farm house. They are now with Denise, where they will forever remain, since I wouldn't dream of taking them away from her, as the older sibling, the honor of being keeper of this very special family legacy. Now, please don't get me wrong, I loved my father, but we are all in agreement that sometimes he went overboard. My poor mom! What she must've gone through in order to put up with the constant stream of wrecked, antique cars to be rebuilt; the helicopter he built in 1968 instead of investing in the houses that were up for sale for closing costs because the builder went bankrupt; the stereo he constructed; or the time he took our only television apart so that he could build a computer. Not to mention his favorite colors, which were yellow, orange, and red. I dare you to try and decorate a house with that color scheme.

If your husband is wanting to come home and redo the kitchen cabinets, rebuild the latest junked car, or landscape the yard by blocking your view with his latest brainstorm, it must either be boredom or testosterone that brings about this urge in a man to create. Notice I said create, not procreate, as this is an entirely new subject.

Epilogue

Some Final Thoughts On Marriage

Ten years. I have been with the same wonderfully exasperating man for ten years. Fourteen, if you count the early years of our relationship, when we were dating. We have had our ups and our downs and our clashes over some unbelievably ludicrous topics. He was my "inspiration" for this book, bless his annoying little heart. It couldn't have been written without him. Or to be more accurate, it couldn't have been written if I hadn't had to suffer the irritation and aggravation of each and every one of his bad habits.

I am not against marriage, mind you. As a matter of fact I am all for it. Would I do it again? Absolutely. With a few changes.

First, I would declare, by way of a written agreement, a no-farting zone. A safe zone if you please. I might even go so far as to design a sign to mark the zone: Picture your hubby's backside, circled in red, with a red, diagonal slash going through it. Keep in mind that this would only work at home, and unless you choose to carry that sign everywhere you go with him, he will probably retaliate, usually in public, for putting a stop to this favored activity. One can only hope that the surgeon general declares methane gas harmful to your health, but, just like smokers, this behavior is probably a form of addiction, so without major therapy (Farter's Anonymous, or possibly a methane patch?) you won't be able to stop him. With men, what goes in must come out, especially when they have an audience.

Burps fall under the same category (almost) as farts. In order to make this delightful pastime livable, I would declare a moratorium on all of the places he is not allowed to belch: Dinner tables, public places, and the bedroom for starters. I would further extend the moratorium to include the types of burps that are not allowed in my presence. Included would be the juicy burp, the straight-from-the-stomach burp, the sulfur burp, and last, but definitely not least, the near-puke burps. Just to name a few.

As for anniversaries, birthdays, and other forgettable events, I would make the penalties so severe that he will never forget to celebrate a single milestone. What about no sex for a month for each forgotten occasion? Provided you can hold out, that is, this may be an effective technique. Considering that he usually forgets them all, it will be well past the millennium before he gets lucky again. This should clear up that problem quickly.

Annoying habits, bad jokes, and public embarrassments will take more finesse on your part. Personally, I have started magnifying my most annoying habit, so that he gets a taste of his own medicine. If it's the butt scratching that's getting on my one remaining nerve, then I will just do what annoys him the most, over and over and over. It also helps to imitate him. This gives him an idea of just how moronic he looks. One morning, I got up and stood by the side of the bed and, scratching, mimicked him. He got all upset and whined, "Now *stop* that!" So I repeated back, "Now stop that!" and so on and so forth. It worked, for a time anyway. Then his short-term memory failed and he went right back to butt scratching. To date, I haven't gotten up the nerve to yell, "Allll righty then!" to every store clerk that I come into contact with, and as for talking through my butt hole, I am not that desperate to make a point.

His cooking techniques might improve with time. If not there are always long, leisurely dinners out, to soften the blow. Or to keep you from blowing chunks. Housekeeping will always be an age-old battle, so unless this is really important to your perfectionist side, you have two choices: accept it for what it is or go on strike and let him live with the mess. The similarities between men and babies will never change. They will never fully grow up, so don't expect any behavior from him that you wouldn't expect from a three year old. In this department miracles will not happen. As for culture, his is what he is, so unless you are a glutton for punishment, I wouldn't even go there. Home improvement stores will always be there to take our hard-earned money, and our husband's time, as long as there are men to frequent them, and wives who continue to despise them.

Now for some good news. There are some areas that we might be able to change. Take for instance the nose, back and ear hair problem. Most men, when it comes to their appearance, are more vain than we are. They will primp and preen for hours in their mistaken reverie of looking like they did at seventeen. In their blindness, they often overlook those wayward hairs that are so repulsive. Therefore, we can make some gentle suggestions as to how they can improve their appearance. This won't solve any behavior problems, especially in public—but, hey, if he looks fantastic maybe people will overlook his personality. Who knows? It's worth a try. Decorating is another area, if approached tactfully, we can work on. Breakdancing fads fade away, and giant whiskey bottles soon get replaced with baby bottles. Over time, as the good old days of bachelorhood fade, he will become more agreeable to letting those treasures fade with it.

Even though we get exasperated with our guys, I wouldn't trade mine for a million bucks. Differences aside, he can always be counted on to ruffle my feathers. And when I start to get aggravated, I simply dust off the decade old memory of my Purina Dog Chow back pack, which makes me realize that I could do much worse. He might always be a Jim Carrey imitating, butt-scratching cheapskate, but he *is* mine, and I look forward to many more decades of horror stories to tell, ruffled feathers.

Thanks, Tim, for the memories!